Lola Love

L'il Miss Bliss

Love and leopard-print tents to...

All the Pink Ladies who read the books and visit the website – Lola and I ADORE you!
Susie – thanks for reminding me that we have to 'go through the process'
and for being the most fabulous-o BFF – mwoahh!
Ed-girl Lindz – for having pretty shoes and handbags – oh,
and for being good with words too, obv.
Miss Aimee – you're a totes inspir-o girl! I love our PJ-wearing,
late night goss sessions and fabu trips to Par-ee – ooh la la!
Thanks for always being there and for being my partner in sass!
Adam and Vicky – for letting me hang at yours when life gets sucky
and for lending me Billy-dog for walks, hugs and accessorising!
Martin – shalom! The land o' potatoes is lucky to have you
and your facial hair – miss you, like, all the time.
Richie Peps – for film watching, garlic bread eating and being every kind of awesome.
Brettster – God, she's not jukebox Cyndi, y'know – I heart you!
Anthony, Martyn and gorgeous agent-lady Bex for the 411 on festivities
and The Piperita Patties – you freakin' rock and rule – grazie!

First published in the UK by HarperCollins Children's Books in 2009

1 3 5 7 9 10 8 6 4 2

ISBN 13: 978-0-00-731064-7

A CIP catalogue record for this title is available from the British Library.

Printed and bound in Great Britain

L'il
Miss Bliss

HarperCollins *Children's Books*

Chapter One

The Bliss Weekender

Chamomile Park, Rockbury
1st and 2nd August
Rock out. Dance. Chill. Smile.
Welcome to a weekend of bliss-kissed awesomeness!

Saturday
Kelk and The Skinny Jeanz
The Piperita Patties
The Hotsters feat. Ryan&James
Ooh-la-la Aimee
Do You Want A Kipper Before You Leave, Kelly?
The Heike/Cross Love Project
Cleaver
Seek Don't Heidi

Sunday
The Tootie
Peploss At The Movies
The Boxall Billydogs
The Notorious BBB
Browner Rules OK
Martin the Great
This Ain't Your Mother's Book Club
The Stokes

Plus exciting events and happening happenings – fashion shows, acoustic sets, drumming workshops, meditation, holistic health clinic, crystal healing, tarot card reading, plus lots, lots more...

"Lola, come check out this line-up!" Bella says in a pitch that could shatter glass. I drag my black bin bag of trashy treasures that I'm collecting for today's Rumble in the Jumble – the local jumble sale that the Pink Ladies and I have a stall at – and pretend to be interested.

"Mmm," I say, not even glancing at the poster. "Looks cool."

The Bliss Weekender is famous for being one of those hippy-dippy festivals, the kind where people walk around in silly costumes, make peace signs at each other and dance to obscure music. Now, while Bella might be used to that kinda thing, what with Yoga Dad being a bit...y'know, hippy-dippy himself, I am finding it hard to muster up a whole lot of non-existent excitement for Zen Dens and bands that I've probably never, ever heard of. No one cool ever plays the Bliss Weekender – even I know that and I've never even been to a festival.

"Seriously Lo, it's crazy-awesome!" Bella says, seemingly oblivious to my total lack of interest. "Ooh-la-la Aimee AND Kelk and The Skinny Jeanz? In the same line-up? I mean, how amazing is that?!"

"Amazing," I say, returning to the much more exciting job of clearing my space of trash to make room for cute new treasure.

Bella, in an extended version of totally-out-of-character excitement, nearly loses her chewing gum as she continues to drool over the Bliss Weekender advert in her latest issue of *Lyrix* magazine. *Lyrix*, unlike *Missy*, my magazine of choice, is read by only the most achingly cool hipster-types. Which is why I'm slightly surprised that they're even running an advert for the Bliss Weekender, what with the fest being the very opposite of all things cool. Like the magazine, Bella is 'achingly cool' personified. In case you're in any doubt as to her Cool Carol credibility, today, in preparation for Rumble in the Jumble, she is working an all-black goth-girl ensemble with her platinum blonde hair backcombed to within an inch of its life and a slick of blood red lip stain. It's a look I'd describe as horror-deluxe – although not to her face – yet despite all the ways it should be wrong, it's really, really right.

"Seriously Lo," Bella says, catching the gum with her tongue, "Ooh-la-la Aimee is the most influential woman in British music right now. She just gets it, y'know?!"

To be honest, I don't know.

I know Ooh-la-la Charlie, our boy-pal of Français loveliness who Bella works with at the weekend, but Ooh-la-la Aimee? Nope – although I'm pretty sure she's on one of the playlists Bella has been blasting out at me morning, noon and night. What I definitely do know is never to stop Bella mid-convo when discussing her much-varied collection of fave muso-girls, so I stop filling the bin liner with unwanted shoes and jewellery, kick off my pink Converse and settle back into my pillows for an education in muso-girl, given by my very own punk princess of muso-girls herself, Miss Bella. Whether I like it or not.

"She takes risks, Lo, and that's so important. Not just with her music but with her outfits too... Look!" Bella flicks to page 26 of *Lyrix*, and holds up a picture of Ooh-la-la Aimee on stage for me to look at.

And I have to admit, Bella's right. It's complete factuality: this girl rocks. Big, big curly hair, drawn-on-with-felt-tip glasses, an all-in-one red and white sailor suit and white knee-high socks with red frill trim, worn with six inch killer platform heels.

"Wow," I say, stretching across the bed to get a better look. "I might not have heard her music, but I'm definitely developing a may-jah girl crush based on her outfit-putting-together ability."

Bella, suitably pleased with my response, continues her Ooh-la-la Aimee 101. "And she's totally not afraid to say what she thinks even if it gets her into trouble, she looks increds, and basically, she's gonna be a total icon of our times, Lo! And guess what else?"

Now, there's nothing I'd like more than to indulge Bella in a l'il guessing game type scenario, but she knows that until two minutes ago I wasn't even aware of Ooh-la-la Aimee's existence, so the chances of me being able to guess anything about her are going to be purr-itty slim.

"She's playing The Pier?" I suppose it's only polite to try.

"Way better. We," Bella says, in a very high pitch that I'd expect from Pink Lady, Sadie, *not* my Cool Carol Americano hipster, Bella, "are actually going to meet her!" Bella squeezes her eyes together really tight and does a celebratory air-punch in the way only an Americano can.

"We are?" I ask, pulling my face into a shape that I'm hoping resembles as much excitement as Bella's actually feeling. "When? Where? And more importantly, how the applesauce did you make *that* happen?"

"You're not going to believe this, Lo-Lo," she says, taking both my hands in hers and pulling me to my feet. "Dad has been asked to do some yoga workshops at the Bliss Weekender, and one of his clients is Ooh-la-la Aimee's manager!"

"Ohhh, I see," I say, except I don't – not really. Bella knows that festivals are not how this pink-haired chica rolls. As much as I love music, the idea of holing up in a tent, surrounded by mud, without so much as a hairdryer for three days? I think not. And yet, from what I'm hearing right now, Bella seems to be suggesting that there is indeed some kind of festival-type set-up on the cards, and that the aforementioned set-up will involve me.

"Wait, that's not even the best bit!" Bella says, and I breathe a silent sigh of relief, because the idea of Bella and I having to share a tent with Yoga Dad at a hippy-dippy festival is nothing like my idea of a best bit. "Pops has arranged for all of us – me, you and your mum – to go along for the whole weekend! We'll pack up the van, pitch a tent, bake bananas, see awesome bands, get henna tattoos – Lo, it's going to be like the best family-bonding trip ever! Amazing, right?"

No, actually. Not amazing. Think amazing, then think what the very opposite of amazing might be, and then you'll be really, really close to how NOT amazing this situ actually is.

Chapter Two

Reasons why a 'family-bonding' trip to the Bliss Weekender is NOT amazing:

We are NOT a family. Yoga Dad and The Mothership might be an item, but that doesn't mean I have to be cool about it. (And FYI, I'm not. I'm really not. And, quite frankly, neither would you be if you'd come downstairs to find them both doing sun salutations in the

living room. In just their pyjamas. I know:
Icksville, right?)

Since we are NOT a family, we do NOT
need to 'bond'. I don't even talk to my own
dad, let alone bond with someone else's.

The Mothership and I are still very much
new to the whole 'mother/daughter' thing, so
I am not loving the idea of enforced bonding.
Avec Bella and Yoga Dad. In a field. In
the middle of nowhere.

I DO NOT dig the idea of festivals. Don't get
me wrong, I love nothing more than rocking out
to obscure-named bands with my Pink Ladies on
The Pier near my house, but at a festival? It's
not that I don't love the music, but I am very

much like Angel when it comes to the concept of camping. I mean, seriously, where
would I plug my hair straighteners? And
then there's the mud. Let's not even talk
about the mud.

It's not even a cool festival with cute
shaggy-haired guitar boys; it's a hippy-dippy
festival with stilt walkers and falafel and
people in silly hats. There is nothing, I repeat, nothing, to love about that.

Did I mention the mud?

Bella is visibly unimpressed with my lack of enthusiasm for what she thinks is quite possibly the best thing ever to happen, like, ever.

"What's wrong?" she asks, putting her hands on her hips and pulling her trademark pout. "That band you and Sadie are in crush with – The Tootie? They're headlining on the Saturday. And The Piperita Patties, that kick-ass girl band from Italy we discovered on MySpace? They're going to be there too and you totally dig them, right?"

I press the pause button on my grumpy-glum for a moment. The Tootie? The Piperita Patties? I do love them. Both of them. This is certified, actual fact.

"What are they doing playing at an event like the Bliss Weekender?" I ask, leaning over for a better look at the ad whilst trying to pretend I didn't completely ignore it in the first place. "I thought it was just for old hippies like Yoga Da—I mean, well...what I mean is, I didn't think it was for cool bands..."

"Well, Lola Love," Bella pouts, "it just goes to show what you know, doesn't it?" She passes me the advert again and as I scan the line-up I can see that the Bliss Weekender has gone and got itself seven shades of cool.

"The Bliss Weekender is now officially the festival of the summer," Bella chirps, "the tickets sold out in, like, minutes this year and there are tons of people are buying them for crazy money on the internet; we've already got ours! Seriously, I thought you'd be doing freakin' star-jumps, Lo."

"Well," I say, feeling all sorts of unexplainable not-nice emotions bubble up inside me, "I'm not, okay?"

I don't know where this angsty, not-very-pink 'tude is coming from, and I don't particular know that I like it, but no matter how amazing the line-up for the Bliss Weekender is, or how pink I try to think, when I picture a family bonding/Bliss Weekender combo all I can see is a big cloud of dark, grey gloomy-glums.

Bella almost gasps at my out-of-character excitement

no-show, picks up her Heidi Seeker clutch and makes her way to the door.

"Wait!" I sigh, nearly tripping over my previously kicked-off Converse. Bella stops, spins and looks at me like she's waiting to open a big can of super-sized Bella Crazy on my bee-hind, so I hold my hands up in surrender.

"Look, I'm grumpy, okay?" I say. "Which I know is no explanation whatsoever, but..."

"Yeah, you're right, it's so not," Bella interrupts. "And for someone who is meant to be L'il Miss Pink-Thinkin', being grumpy is something you're getting pretty good at lately, Lola Love."

Ouch. That hurt.

Before I even have chance to come up with a response, Bella is channeling her goth-girl ensemble, muttering something about me being 'unbelievably ungrateful' and 'outstandingly selfish' under her breath, and telling me, out loud, that I can make my own way to Rumble in the Jumble.

Now, for someone who is two whole years older and, as she's always so quick to point out, significantly wiser than me, I'm thinking this is a teensy, weensy bit immature, and that she might as well have stuck out her tongue and blown a big, fat raspberry at me. Still, I'm not sure now is the right time to point this out to her.

With the world's biggest and loudest sigh, I throw myself back onto my bed in the style of every silver-screen movie goddess before me, because my life IS a movie (starring me, Lola Love) and should be filled with fabulosity, cupcakes and inexplicable outbursts of song. Fall-out girl dramaramas, hippy-dippy festivals and parental hook-ups should, quite frankly, NOT be in the script. But Bella and I are making quite the habit of falling out lately. It's not like I'm intentionally going out of my way to argue with her, but

I'm afraid to say that what just happened there isn't a new thing in the world of Lola and Bella.

When Bella talked to Yoga Dad about it (because that's what they do; they talk), he said, in his own Americano yoga dude way, that I'm adjusting to change, and because change can be hard, we should just 'chill' and 'hang'. I say I wouldn't have to adjust to change if stuff wasn't happening all around me at lightning speed. Which, FYI Yoga Dad, is all because of you.

It's not that I don't like Yoga Dad – I do. I really do. He and Bella have one of those really cool, talk-about-everything parental set-ups, he talks in super-wise rhymes and riddles and is a bendy-wendy supreme-o who can chill The Mothership out in a record next-to-nanoseconds speed and for that alone I want to kiss his sandal-and-socked feet, but the idea of him being MY Yoga Dad? Well, that positively freaks me out. I mean, it hardly seems like two minutes since my actual dad vanished from our lives, without the ma-parental bringing in a new one. And it's not like The Mothership or Yoga Dad have actually said anything to suggest that's actually happening – ohmystars, I'd hide under my duvet indefinitely if they even so much as tried to talk to me about it right now – but Bella, well, she jokes about it ALL the time. Except it's not a joke, because jokes are meant to be funny, and after I had to single-handedly deal with the eye-scarring that was the The Mothership and Yoga Dad greeting the sun in their bendy-wendy way in PJs, I can 100% certify that right now The Mothership/Yoga Dad collaboration getting all kinds of serious is the most unfunny joke ever.

Chapter Three

"Seriously Lo-Lo, what is it with you two at the moment?" Sadie asks, shaking her head as she picks through my bin bag of soon-to-be-sold treasures. "I can't leave you and Bella alone together for five minutes without you both turning this pink palace into a war zone!"

I shrug my shoulders, not because I don't altogether know what *is* going on with us two at the moment but because I just don't want to talk about it. But I am happy to talk about the fact that Bella left me stranded with two bin bags of jumble swag, which is why I rang Sadie to enlist the help of Scottie-Too-Hottie, her car-driving bro, to help me get them to the Pier. Although, if I'm honest, he's not being much help at all, and is sitting in his car listening to tunes while Sadie and I struggle to shift my swag bags across the landing.

"Ooh," Sadie says, momentarily distracted as she pulls out a bright yellow boom box brooch from a bag of random accessories I've put aside to sell. "Can I have this?"

"Miss Sades, how are we ever going to make money for our Fund O' Summer if you keep nicking the soon-to-be-sold merch?"

This is so typically Sadie. As official events organiser for the

Pink Ladies, it was her idea to start a Fund O' Summer, so that when school was out we'd have fundage for Pink Lady adventures, which, FYI, are the very best kind. Except school is now out, and our Fund O' Summer is still sitting at a big, fat zilcho. So, in true pink-thinking style, Sadie decided that we should all start the summer by becoming de-clutter bunnies. She ordered us, in the nicest possible Sadie-like way of course, to fill up bags with all the things we no longer wanted to sell at the coolest vintage market in town, Rumble in the Jumble.

"But this is so cute, Lo," Sadie pleads, already pinning it to her t-shirt, "and look, it goes so well with my tee... Pleeeeeeease? Please can I have it?!"

"Oh, go on then." I nod my head because she's right: it looks perfect with her super-cute candy pink tee from the kids' department at H&M. "But no more, otherwise we'll have nothing left to actually sell!"

"Deal!" she says, putting her hands on her hips and pulling model-esque poses in my bedroom mirror. "Hey, what's this?" she asks, stopping mid-pose, to de-pin a hand-drawn picture of me dressed as Wonder Woman from my pin board. "*Lola Love – Go-For-It Girl!* – I love it! Did you draw this, Lo-Lo?"

"No," I say, feeling slightly coy and girly all of a sudden, "Oscar sent it to me this morning!"

"Ahhh, the adorable Oscar!" Sadie sighs. "How's he doing?"

"He's cool," I say, trying really hard to stop my smile from spreading beyond my ears and out into the stratosphere some-where. "He says I have to say hi!"

Oscar is my current boy-type of choice and the most amazing thing is that he's real. Seriously. He's not even a pop star or a boy from the TV and he's all kinds of wonderful. Of course, I used to crush on the lovely Jake Farrell, who was the official heir to my heart for a looong time, but then he started dating Evil Eva Satine (boo), and during rehearsals for our last school play, let's just say he turned out to be less than lovely. As in toxic. But Oscar, sweet, cute-as-a-button Oscar, was the first boy to give me flowers (even if they were from my neighbour's garden), to watch the stars with me, help me learn my lines and (blush) give me my first proper kiss. Basically, he's just like the most perfectly formed cupcake of deliciousness – a super-fluffy, melt-your-heart inside, with just the right amount of yummy icing on the outside, finished with a light dusting of magic glitter sprinkles. Sigh.

Tragically, Oscar was only visiting, and had to go home to Ireland and his parentals. Oh, I can't believe I didn't mention his accent.

Sigh.

Thud.

It's bee-you-tiful boy-band Irish, and is positively Swoonsville. Luckily for me, Oscar and are I are both writer-types – he creates cartoon strips and I make zines – so while we can't be everyday hang-out buds anymore, we have channeled our shared love of all things retro and become penpals, using pens and paper and everything – it's so old-school. He is cuteness on a lollystick. Fact.

"Is that it? Are you grumpy because you miss Oscar?" Sadie asks, waving a hand in front of my face to wake me from my distant, moon-eyed, hazy gaze. "Is that what's up, Miss L?"

"Grumpy?" I ask Sadie, slightly confused as to where this line of questioning might be going. "What is it with this whole grumpy business? First Bella, now you! I'm not even grumpy!"

Sadie pulls a 'well, you could have fooled me' face, and I'm shocked, because I'm not grumpy, I'm really not. I'm not my fully-charged pink-thinking self, I admit, but just because life isn't a family-sized box of chocolates right now, doesn't mean I'm having a permanent attack of the Gloomy Grumps. Does it?

"Are you serious?" I ask defensively. 'Do you really think I'm grumpy?"

"Well..." Sadie sighs, "look, we're Pink Ladies, right?"

I nod, because despite the fact that she's accusing me of being grumpy, this is factuality.

"And Pink Ladies don't lie to each other, right?" she continues.

I nod again, as this too is fact, not just for the Pink Ladies, but for all girlkind.

"Okay," Sadie says, with a deep intake of breath, "then yes. Yes, you have been grumpy, and it's just so completely out of character, Lo, that we just don't know how to deal—"

"We?" I interrupt. "Who's *we*? Have you and Bella been talking about me behind my back?"

"No!" Sadie squeals, pulling her pixie-like self across the bed so she can put her hands on my knees. "Not at all, Lo-Lo! We're just worried about you, that's all."

"So you *have* been talking about me?" I start to feel a not-nice emo-overload in my tummy for the second time today. "Pink Ladies DO NOT do that. They do not talk about friends behind their backs!"

I brush her hands from my knees and pull them up close to my chest.

"Lo," Sadie says quietly, "we were genuinely worried. We thought maybe Oscar leaving upset you more than you let on, and we were just trying to work out how we could make you feel better, that's all..."

"No," I reply, trying not to make eye-water, "if I'm grumpy, it's hardly because of Oscar. Maybe next time you and Bella are talking about me, she should ask herself what my problem might be—"

I pause, and just as I'm about to spill to Sadie all the awkwardness and not-niceness I'm feeling about The Mothership and Yoga Dad and how Bella has already written and stamped herself a 'I'm the best step-sister in the world' certificate, I stop myself, because even if my world is turning to broken biscuit, it's not fair to involve Sadie. So I change direction, I take a deep yoga breath, count to ten in my head and pull my mouth into something like the shape of a smile.

"Look," I say, trying to make my voice sound as easy-breezy and not-bothered as possible, "I'm sorry. I know you both care, but I got upset today because, basically, Yoga Dad has got tickets for Bella, the ma-parental and I to go to the Bliss Weekender, and I just don't want to go."

I try really hard to squeeze my pink-socked feet into my still-tied Converse, avoiding any eye contact in the hope that we can just forget all about it and make our way to Rumble in the Jumble.

"What?!" Sadie says, as a look of total horror – the kind that really should be saved for bad, bad people and reality TV shows – takes over her whole face. "Lo, you do realise that the Bliss Weekender is going to be THE festival of the summer, right?"

"Yes," I sigh, realising immediately that Pink Lady, Sadie is completely the wrong person to be looking to for any kind of sympathy based on my not wanting to attend aforementioned festival. "It *has* been brought to my attention."

"And you do realise that The Tootie are headlining on the

Saturday, right?" she asks, searching my face for any kind of sanity, because right now I know she thinks I'm completely mad.

"Again, Miss Sadie," I say, biting my bottom lip to stop myself from feeling any more stressy than I already do, "I have been made aware of this fact too; it's just, as much as I'd love to see The Tootie – *and* The Piperita Patties for that matter – the thought of spending a weekend in a field, in the middle of nowhere, with just Bella, The Mothership and Yoga Dad, well...it just doesn't rock my world."

I stamp around the room making sure my feet are firmly in my trainers, scoop up a bin bag full of to-be-sold merch and stand in my bedroom doorway.

"Are you coming?" I ask, making it clear that this particular convo is well and truly over. "Your bro will be getting mad at us – we've taken forever!"

Sadie shakes her head at me, grabs a carrier and follows me down the stairs.

Chapter Four

By the time we rock up to Rumble in the Jumble, it is clear that between us, we've brought way too much stuff. Angel, having expressed nothing but disgust at having to be involved in anything that even remotely resembles a visit to a chazza shop, has brought an entire trunk of never-been-worn bags and clothes and could easily host a stall all of her own. Meanwhile, Bella, in her typical Bella way, is pretending that our earlier argument didn't actually happen, and right now, to avoid a messy, stressy public situ, I'm more than happy to go along with that. I wouldn't usually, because fronting up is deffo the Think Pink way, but as I've already had cross words with Bella and nearly argued with Sadie, all before 10am on a Sunday morning, I'm thinking *Livin' La Vida Lola* should be less about the fronting, and more about the fun. For today at least.

"Hey ladies," Bella shouts across the hall from behind a teeny-tiny table that she's filling with CDs and DVDs. "So, Angel and I have done our best to merch the space and we're trying super-hard not to spill out onto our lovely neighbours' tables." Bella smiles, putting her arm around the shoulders of a girl who looks just like Louise Brooks, one of those silent film stars of the twenties – all sharp black bob and Cupid's bow lips. She's wearing a red satin forties-style tea dress with matching bright red lips – très cool.

"This is Marie Ann," Bella says, introducing us to the just-stepped-out-of-celluloid girl o' prettiness, "Marie Ann, this is Lola and Sadie!"

"Hey hey," she says, lifting her hand to wave at us. "Wow, you guys have a lot of stuff!"

I look down at the two bin bags and three carriers we've just unloaded from Scottie-Too-Hottie's car, and realise that, yep, she's right, we really do.

"Well," I say, pouring a small bag of badges and brooches into a pink plastic bowl, "it's a shiny Sunday morning, so I'm hoping the sun will bring out all the trashy-treasure-buying hipsters!"

"Fingers crossed!" she says, holding up a perfectly manicured entwined middle and forefinger. Marie Ann is way older than us – older than Bella, maybe in her twenties – and her quirky look and general loveliness makes me feel a big, giant miss-you pang for my Aunt Lullah. They don't look alike, but they have the same kind of awesome-girl-aura about them.

Aunt Lullah lives in NYC, but is currently in Hollywood designing costumes for a new chick flick. Her job is super-swanky, but I love that she's just as much at home on a film set as she is watching Audrey movies and eating ice-cream from the tub with me.

Marie Ann is having a wardrobe clear-out: there's everything from *faux*-fur coats to denim skirts of varying lengths, and randomly and right at the end of the rail is a pale blue ball gown with a gazillion little crystals sparkling across its front. I nudge Sadie and point to the dress; she gives me a knowing glance, and asks Marie Ann how much it is.

"Fiver?" Marie Ann says. "My sister made me wear it at her wedding. It's horrific, isn't it?"

Sadie and I both laugh: while her selling technique definitely needs a little bit of work, she's adorable, so Sadie buys it anyway. I have no doubt that her customising ways can – and will – turn the 'horrific' bridesmaid dress into something prom-like and beyond fabulous.

To our left are the self-titled Glitter Gals, who have a cute home-made promo sign above a heaving rail of second-hand clothing and a table of bric-a-brac heaven, and next along is a stall selling vintage trading cards and novelty jewellery.

As soon as the doors open at 11am, the Pier Ballroom is filled to the brim with elbow-sharp treasure hunters, and any earlier bad feeling there might have been between the Pink Ladies is now totally forgotten, because together, we are having quite possibly the best fun ever.

Sadie has designed and printed up some fake cupcake tattoos and has a queue of sweet-looking girls who want to be a little bit rock star but still oh-so-adorable, and her customised gingham rosettes, in a variety of candy colours, are proving to be very popular. She's so going to be a top designer one day.

Bella is talking to some skinny-jean-wearing hipster boys with matching super-preened yet madly messy hairdos about how totally underrated *Mr. Obscuro* really is. Her muso-knowledge, combined with flutter-by mascara-ed eyelash-batting, is making her a skirty-flirty force of fierceness: she's already sold nearly half of the CDs she brought with her in under half an hour.

Even Angel is embracing her inner thrift-girl, and is selling an entire carrier bag full of never-been-worn Angel treasure to a really loud, super-tall, well-dressed Chinese dude who is wearing thick-rimmed black glasses.

"Sweetie," he shouts, searching in his Prada man bag, "you're an absolute lifesaver! Please, take my card – I LOVE you; you have such an eye for style – call me!"

Angel puffs up her afro with pride and Fashionista Boy scoops in for two obligatory fashion world air-kisses, turning to blow her another as he leaves the ballroom. Angel, a seasoned pro, tilts her head to one side and blows him one back.

"Who was *that*?" Sadie and I ask in unison, trying to get a look at the card she's holding out in front of her.

"That, girls," Angel says, puffing at her 'fro some more, "was Chris Huang, fashion stylist to the stars!"

"Nooooo!" Sadie gasps. "What's he doing here?"

In response to the 'who-the-applesauce-is-that?' face I'm pulling, Sadie briefly explains that Chris Huang is big news in fashion and that all the new music acts and magazines are fighting for him to work with them. Angel, bored with the back-story, is impatient to fill us in on the main event.

"So," Angel whispers, as if she is about to impart the most salacious of gossip, "they're doing a shoot on the beach with that new dance act, Miss Ce-Ce? But apparently she is being a diva of epic proportions, and won't wear any of the clothes Chris has brought with him, but luckily for him, I had some neon-fabulous ensembles – designer, of course – that he has just bought for £100!"

"Ohmystars! No way!" I shout. "£100? That's amazing, Angel – you're amazing!"

"I know, Lola," she says, letting out a dramatic sigh, "I know!"

Chapter Five

Business slows right down after lunch, so I take a quick skip around the place. Surely the whole point of having a clear-out is that I can then buy lots of lovely new things to fill my empty space with, *non*? There are stalls both upstairs and downstairs selling the best second-hand and vintage clothing, records, awesome junk, sunglasses, badges, jewellery and trading cards along with homemade cupcakes (of which I buy and eat two – they aren't Sadie-standard, obvs, but they're still really good) and anything else you can think of. I can't see him, but somewhere there's a rad DJ playing '60s soul music that makes me want to shake my bee-hind.

Sadie's been working really hard on some cute, big-bow head-bands that she's selling on our stall, and I've seen at least three girls wearing them – it makes my heart fill with total pride and love stuff for my super-talented, creative gal-pal; so much so that I buy a knitted cupcake from a red-haired girl who is knitting her woollen treats as she sells, and plan to make it into a celebratory brooch for her. I also purchase a pink and white hula-hoop – be-cause everyone knows that hula-hooping, retro-girl style, is THE only way to keep fit – a black tote bag with a pink typewriter on the front – a total must-have for a zine making, writer-girl like myself

– and I bagsy a beaten-up copy of a book called *Star Girl* by Jerry Spirelli (from amongst a heap of crime novels and other bric-a-brac craziness) that I just simply have to own. It has a pink cover and on the back, the blurb reads: *'She was the faintest scent of a cactus flower'*. Mucho intriguing...

I arrive back at our stall, which, compared to those around us, is now looking decidedly bare, to find Angel, Bella and Sadie with their heads together in a slightly conspiratorial we're-up-to-something type way.

"Hey ladies," I say, standing in front of the table with my hula-hoop in one hand and a tote bag full of goodies in the other, "whassup?"

They look up, one after the other, with identical pleased-with-themselves grins across all three of their bee-you-tiful yet so very different faces. Bella nudges Angel, and Angel, puffing at her 'fro for what must be the 84th time today, stands up and steps round the table to join me.

"Miss Lola Love," she says, linking her arm with mine and walking me around to where Bella and Sadie are standing, "we've been thinking..."

Oh.

Thinking, you say.

Are you sure you don't mean talking?

About me?

I give her a look but it doesn't stop her. Nothing can stop Angel once she's started. Except maybe a fifty percent off designer shoe sale.

I should have known that this would happen. Bella and Sadie think I've got a permanent case of the grumpy-glums, so they've enlisted Miss Angel, *my* BFF, the only one they know I can't and won't be mad at, to talk to me about it. Which is *really* unfair, because I haven't even been that grumpy – although if I *had* been, I would've had absolutely every right to be.

So there.

"Woah there, Groucho Marx," Angel says, pulling at my arms, which have automatically folded across my chest, and prodding at my smile, which has turned to a scowl. "At least hear me out before you start throwing the 'don't-mess-with-me' body language, please..."

I want to laugh out loud at Angel calling me 'Groucho Marx', because it's quite clear I'm *not* some old comedy dude with a black moustache. But I don't.

I drop the arms, but I still throw all my body weight onto one hip and tilt my head to form what I think is a pretty convincing 'come on then, give me what you got' pose.

"Look, Lo-Lo," Angel says, shaking her head at what she knows is my poor attempt at bad-girl 'tude, "Bella has mentioned that you weren't so cool about the whole 'festival' idea..."

Ahhh. The Bliss Weekender.

Again.

At least this time round I know Angel will feel my pain. She might have agreed to attend a jumble sale, but there is no way in the world she would ever get her cute-as-a-button self dirty at a festival. Fact.

"So as you know, Miss Lola, the rules of Angel state: never put yourself in a situation where you cannot be fabulous 100% of the time, and under normal circumstances, you know I'd be right there with you, hating on the whole festival idea, right?"

I nod, not altogether liking the idea that my fact may possibly be about to turn to fiction.

"But Lo, seriously, this year the Bliss weekender is THE festival to go to..."

"Really?" I snap, annoyed that the one person I thought I could rely on for support in any kind of hippy-dippy/mud avoidance situ has gone and signed up to the 'I heart festivals' fan club too. "That's funny, because no, I hadn't heard."

Angel shoots me a glare and takes a deep breath. "Well anyway," she continues, "all the fashion magazines are talking about it. Vivienne Sui is even doing a catwalk show there, which means the whole place will literally be heaving with fashionista-types..."

"And your point is?" I shrug, knowing exactly what her point is, but wanting to hear it from her own lip-glossed mouth, because I can't quite believe that my BFF, L'il Miss High-Maintenance Stylista, is *actually* hinting that she would *actually* want to go to the Bliss Weekender.

"My point is, Miss Sassypants," Angel says, checking my 'tude, "we all really want to go."

"Apart from me, remember..." I interrupt. "I really *don't* want to go." I look at them all as I say it, just to make sure they're all completely clear about that.

"Will you at least hear me out, Lo?" Angel asks. I feel bad, because I really don't know why I'm being so 'tude-y, and if I'm going to be 'tude-y at anyone, it really shouldn't be my Pink Ladies, especially not Angel. I nod at her to continue.

"So, beautiful Bella has spoken to Yoga Dad, who has spoken to the peeps he's going to be working with at the festival, and..."

Angel, as always when telling a story she's particularly pleased with, pauses for dramatic effect. "... He's managed to work his karmic magic, and got two extra tickets!"

"Ohhh-kay..." I say, because I'm not altogether too sure what else *to* say.

"Which means," Angel says, filling in the blanks, "the Pink Ladies – you, me, Bella and Sadie – are going to do the Bliss Weekender together! Our first summer adventure – how amazing is that?!"

Why does everyone keep saying that? In my head, the idea of a festival is far from amazing. It's not amazing. Not one little bit, especially when it involves an enforced family situ. But – and this is a VERY big but – this new very Think Pink slant on a not-very-good idea does seem slightly more do-able. Maybe a teeny tiny little bit more workable in my mind. The Rumble in the Jumble is proof that when all the Pink Ladies do something together, not only do we rock and rule at it, but we have fun too, so I suppose that if I was ever going to do a festival, then I would only ever want to do it as part of a pink-feather-boa-wearing, gal-gang of awesomeness: all four of us, together.

"Lo-Lo," Sadie says, tugging awkwardly at her tee, "I know the idea of going to this festival isn't filling your world with glitter and sparkles right now..."

I stick out my bottom lip and shrug my shoulders. I feel a tiny bit silly admitting that I might not altogether mind going to the Bliss Weekender if we're all going. So I just let her carry on talking.

"But you remember that poster that Oscar made you?" she asks, putting both hands in her jean skirt pockets to stop herself from fiddling with the hem of her tee. "He drew you as a go-for-it girl, right? That's because you *are*, Lo. All the Pink Ladies are – it's how we roll. I mean, how will we ever become totally kick-ass if we don't take risks or push ourselves to try new things and have new experiences?"

Eventually I nod, because I know she's right. Even the ma-parental is more go-for-it girl than me right now. She's eating sushi, doing sun salutations and now she's going to a festival; all these things are so far removed from her comfy zone, yet she's still doing them. And while I might not be 100% cool with the new fam situ, I do know that since she started trying new things, she's been a much nicer version of The Mothership to be around.

"Lo," Sadie continues, linking her petite little hand with mine, "it's just two nights in a tent, that's all. And who knows? You might end up completely loving it – but you'll never know unless you at least give it a go, will you?"

I let out a tiny smile for Sadie. It's hard not to; she has that kind of effect on you. She's like a fairy princess, sprinkling smiles and feel-good happiness wherever she goes.

"And c'mon," Sadie says, ending her pink-tinted speech with maximo impact, "we're the Pink Ladies! Anything we do together will be the most fun ever, right?"

"Right," I agree. Okay, so I don't know how I'm going to keep my candy-pink locks poker-straight, or how I'm going to deal with no access to real, clean toilets for three days, but I do know that I love my gal-pals very, very much, and our adventures are always of the totally fabulous variety.

"Okay, fine," I say, holding my hands up high. "Let's do it, let's get Blissed!"

Chapter Six

"Are you absolutely sure?" I quiz Angel, as we lie in my garden under the shade of the pink parasol. Both of us know that the sun, as pretty as it is, gives you wrinkles, and we do not want wrinkles.

"Lo," she begins, taking a sip of the coconut whip concoction I made her on arrival, "*you* know – more than anyone – that the very idea of a festival is enough to make me want to wail and run for clean sanitation, but after I read about how fashion-forward the whole event is going to be in *Fierce* magazine, with celebrities and catwalk shows, I was like, if it's good enough for the fash pack, it's good enough for me. AKA, future queen of said fash pack."

"But Angel," I remind her, "the current fash pack will have access to clean toilets, nice comfy beds in trailers and power points where they can charge their phones and plug in their hair straighteners. We, on the other hand, will be camping. I repeat, camping. And camping is not the pursuit of high-maintenance girls like us."

"Jeez Louise," Bella's voice shouts from across the garden fence, "quit the festival trash talk will you, Lo? It's going to be so much fun, I absolutely promise. Here, I have something that might make it a whole lot more bearable for you – come and give me a hand."

I jump up from the blanket hoping that Bella has bought a

suitably pink trailer, complete with electricity, running water, and four comfy beds. Now *that* would definitely make it more bearable. But despite being big, the package is deffo not trailer-sized – shame. It is, however, beautifully wrapped in pink paper and tied with a big red bow.

"Wow! What is it?" I ask, lifting the parcel over the fence.

"Wait a minute, and you'll find out!" she says, taking a run-up and jumping our garden fence like an Olympic hurdler – except instead of landing herself a gold medal, she's just landed in The Mothership's flower bed. I'd suggest using the front door, but ever since Bella became my punk-princess next-door neighbour, she's never used conventional entry methods. She still shimmies up the drainpipe to visit me in my pink palace, and while I've explained the modern concept of doors to her at least a hundred times, she never listens.

"Open it then," she shouts, prodding at me impatiently. "If this doesn't make you smile, I don't know what will!"

"Is it twelve mobile phones?" Angel asks in all seriousness, peeking over my shoulder. "I mean, we're not going to be able to charge them up are we? So surely we'll need one for each day..."

"Chill," Bella coos, holding a 'wait-up' palm of calm to Angel. "We've got emergency chargers than you can put your phone battery into, coz dad needs to be contactable at all times – but even if we didn't, the big phone companies have tents where you can charge up your phone for free, and they have a DJ too, so you can sit or dance to cool tunes while it charges..."

"No way!" Angel grabs at my arm. "Lolo, this just gets better and better – it's going to be like living in the real world, but outside!"

"What about my hair straighteners?" I ask hopefully. "Will they have anywhere for me to plug those in?"

"Sadly not, princess," Bella says, stroking my candy-pink locks, "but luckily for you, you have a Bella who will be your on-hand stylist for the entire weekend to make sure you're fest-ready at all times, 'k?!"

Not wanting to be completely ungrateful, I give her a thumbs-up. It's not quite the same but it'll have to do.

"Now come on," Bella says, a little more forcefully this time, "will you open the parcel already?!"

I pull at the bow, which Angel takes and ties in her 'fro, then rip at the paper to discover quite possibly the coolest pink leopard-print tent I have ever seen.

"Ohmystars!" I squeal. "This is amazing! Thanks Bella, you're a superstar!"

"Well," Bella says, visibly pleased to finally get a positive reaction out of me, "Pops said that now there are so many of us going, it makes sense that he and your mom sleep in the camper van, and we get a tent of our own, so I chose this especially for you!"

I read the instructions and see that it sleeps four, next to which Bella has written, in biro, 'Pink Ladies'.

I can't believe that after all the fuss I've been making about not wanting to go to the Bliss Weekender, both Yoga Dad and Bella are going out of their way to make it as pain-free and fun as it can possibly be for me. My inner brat has been ruling my head for the last couple of weeks and it's about time she got back in the playpen. If Angel, the most high-maintenance person I know, is willing to embrace all things festival, then really, so should I. I can at least try, right?

"Okay," I say, sitting up straight to show Bella I mean business. "So, who's playing, what are we going to do, who are we going to see?"

"Well," Bella smiles, rummaging in her new bag, which is in the shape of a pair of big red lips with an across-the-body strap, "I've circled events and acts that we might all like to see..."

She finally pulls out the advert for the Bliss Weekender and flattens it out on the grass.

"Lo, now I know you and Sadie are all about The Tootie, and we'll all want to see The Piperita Patties, but I also think you're just going to love The Stokes – their lyrics are so sarcastic and funny and the lead singer is this really petite red-head who's married to Adam, the lead singer of Cleaver – y'know, the guy with all the tattoos?"

I nod, because I'm vaguely aware of who she's talking about; living next door to Bella is an education in lots of things – hair products, unusual room entry, spirituality – but of course, most importantly, music, so it'd be crazy if some of her big-brain music know-how hadn't rubbed off on me.

"Anyway, I've marked other bands you might like too. The Notorious BBB is really good, and y'know, he's quite hot too – well, if you dig that whole shaggy-haired, old-school Luke Skywalker kind of look. Oh, and Peploss at the Movies is this really cute dude who looks like the kid from the Haribo packets, and he play really adorable songs that should be on a mixtape you'd make for your crush..."

"Sounds cool!" I say, actually feeling the first genuine spark of excitement about the whole festival scenario. "What do you think, Angel?"

"Well, no offence, Bells," Angel begins, "it all sounds really good, but I just NEED to be front row at that Vivienne Sui show on Saturday, so as long as we arrive on time for that, that's all I really care about. I wonder who will be there? I wonder who'll be modelling..."

We have now lost Angel to a hazy montage of designer ensembles and celeb faces in her mind.

"I'm going to go get a drink," Bella says, shaking her head and pulling herself to her big black-booted feet. "You'll have the best time, Lo-Lo, I promise! Everyone has to go to at least one festival before they're twenty – it's practically a law of life!"

I watch Bella sass her way down the garden path, and wonder if it really would be all kinds of awful to have Pink Lady, Bella as a big sister. I mean, it could be a whole lot worse, couldn't it? Mum could be dating someone who is zero on the coolness scale and he might have a daughter who's a cookie cut-out of Evil Eva Satine – ohmystars, that really would be the worst.

So why is it, then, that when Angel and I decide to go to town to buy some last-minute festival must-haves – wet wipes; can you believe we nearly forgot wet wipes? – and I see Bella sitting at the kitchen table, sipping chamomile tea with Yoga Dad and The Mothership, my belly ties itself up in a series of really complicated knots that feel like they'll be virtually impossible to undo?

"Thanks so much for blagging us tickets to the Bliss Weekender," Angel says, heading over to Yoga Dad and giving his shoulders a squeeze. "You're the best!"

"No problem," Yoga Dad smiles, tapping Angel's hand. "I just hope you girls have fun!"

He turns to extend the smile to me. It's warm and sincere, and his eyes crinkle at the sides into tried-and-tested lines. He really is the nicest man, and he makes The Mothership smile too, which nearly never happened before he arrived, but still the knots in my tummy stay tight as I watch this new family set-up play out in front of me like a TV show. Angel is making wide eyes at me, and it's then that I realise that while I'm usually the epitome of politeness, I've not thanked Yoga Dad for the tickets either.

"Oh," I say, trying to loosen my belly knots so I can actually talk, "I'm so sorry, yes, thank you – and thank you for the cool tent too – it's awesome!"

It *is* a cool tent. It's just that I'd be much happier sleeping in it in my back garden instead, that's all. I could have my very own faux-stival, and listen to my fave bands on an mp3 player, with access to unlimited electricity, running water and nice toilets. Now *that* is my kind of festival.

"Ahh, Lola," Yoga Dad says, holding his smile and giving me an almost-wink, "Bella mentioned that you're not a huge fan of camping, but I hope now that you've got all your Pink Ladies in tow, you'll be able to enjoy yourself."

"Well, we'll definitely be more comfortable now we've got a super-cute deluxe tent!" I smile. And I think it almost looks real.

"Being comfortable is overrated," Yoga Dad laughs. "You've got to get *un*comfortable, Lola – start exploring emotions and activities that make you feel weird."

"What?" I ask, not altogether sure I agree with him, because I like comfy. Comfy is good. It's warm and it's familiar.

"As soon as you start to explore the unknown, it becomes the known and you've grown. You've just got to go with the flow, Lola, and if an opportunity to try something new comes along, grab it!"

"So what you're saying is," Angel frowns, trying to untangle Yoga Dad's words of wisdom, "that new experiences help us to learn and grow, and that learning and growing is the stuff that makes us kick-ass?"

"I don't think I said 'kick-ass' but yes, Angel, you've got it," Yoga Dad says, nodding his head in approval. Angel, substantially pleased with herself, holds her hand up for a high five. I shake my head and tap her hand.

"So hey," I say, turning to Bella, who is showing The Mothership a picture of a girl with tattoos, "Angel and I are going to town: if I'm going to learn and grow at the Bliss Weekender, I'm going to need pink wellie boots and a matching pink rain mac to do it in. You want to come, Bella?"

"No, that's cool, thanks," Bella says, taking another sip of tea and making herself comfy, "I think I'm just going to hang here. I'm trying to talk your mom into having a henna tattoo with us at the fest, Lo-Lo!"

"Really?" I ask, feeling another new knot forming in my tummy – except this one feels like it's the size of an entire house. "Well, good luck with that!"

"Oh you never know. I think we both need to get a little bit uncomfy, don't you, Lola?" the ma-parental says, grabbing my hand and squeezing it.

"Mmmm," I mutter, "maybe..." Although, if I'm honest, I'm feeling more uncomfy now than I've felt in a long time, and I'm not altogether sure that I like it too much.

Chapter Seven

"Road trip!" Bella sings up the stairs. "Lola, we're going on a road trip!"

Of course it's not just a road trip. It's a road trip to a festival. A festival I am still not 100% sold on. But Bella, despite her own over-brimming excitement for all things fest, is being a total doll and going out of her way to make sure my first festival experience is a good one and I, Lola Love, hand on heart do solemnly swear to try and put my tummy knots and Gloomy Grumps away for the entirety of the Bliss Weekend.

Now, while I might not be doing somersaults and cartwheels at the idea of mud-covered fresco living, it is true that there is nothing I heart more than a road trip. My mum and my dad can't drive, so most of my childhood was spent either on a bus or on the handlebars of my dad's bike, which means I'm always beside myself at the slightest hint that I might be heading out of town in a cool set of wheels. One day, I plan on travelling from one side of America to the other, with a suitcase of vintage-style frocks, wearing a Marilyn-esque headscarf, in a drop-top pink 1950s Cadillac – how Swoonsville would that be? Now that's my idea of a road trip.

"I've even made a mix-tape!" Bella says as she runs up the stairs, "like before CDs and mp3 playlists were invented!"

"I know what a cassette is, Bell!" I tut, stuffing my fourth pair of shoes into my fit-to-burst pink holdall. "Why didn't you just burn a CD? Wouldn't it have been easier?"

"The CD player in the camper van has broken," Bella informs me, prodding around my holdall, "so we're going to kick it old school! Ah, Lo, why have you got FOUR pairs of shoes?"

"Well," I begin, willing to defend my fashion choices to the death while Bella pulls out the pair I've just stuffed in there, along with the first, second and third pairs too.

"Seriously, you don't need all these – especially these," she says, holding up my gorgeous pair of pink kitten heels with big red satin bows on the front. "It's a festival, Lola!"

"But if we're going to go to a fashion show while we're there, Bells," I plead, "then I'll need to look suitably stylish!"

"But Lo," Bella begins, "there's no point in taking anything that you really love – things can get lost, get ruined if it rains..."

"Well in that case," I interrupt, "I might as well just empty my case!" I don't want to admit it but she's totally right.

Bella starts to laugh but her smile turns to an expression of complete shock as she looks out the window. "You have got to be kidding me!" she says, shaking her head in disbelief.

The thing is, if Bella thought my packing skills were bad, then she had not reckoned on Miss Angel Trueman trumping me. Big time.

I join Bella at the window and can't help but laugh as my gorgeous gal-pal Angel makes her way down my garden path with a bright yellow pull-case, two holdalls, a Hello Kitty backpack, a vanity case AND an across the shoulder sparkly red heart purse, thrown together with a low-key ensemble that consists of a vivid violet jumpsuit and '80s style kicks with neon green laces. I love Angel Trueman.

As I run downstairs to let her in, Bella runs right behind me, not even letting Angel through the door before taking her two holdalls from her hands.

"You two, " Bella demands, "follow me!"

I hug Angel and roll my eyes at Bella's bossy ways.

"What's up with her?" Angel asks, looking a little bit put out.

When it comes to fashion, Angel is the supreme 'bossy one' and doesn't take too kindly to other people – especially Bella – threatening to wear her bossy boots better than she does. And yes, they're designer; you'd expect nothing less, would you?

"What's up, Angel," Bella barks, pulling Angel's case flat onto my bedroom floor and unzipping it, "is that you and Miss Sassy-Pants here think you're going on a two week holiday to freakin' Spain..."

If only, I mutter under my breath, *if only*.

"That is not true," Angel says, pulling at the 1950s-style floral playsuit that Bella is trying to put in a stay-at-home pile. "I don't have nearly enough here for two whole weeks."

And she's not even kidding. Angel's look of confusion and my stifled giggles do not amuse Miss Bella.

Sensing Bella's stressy messy head, Angel starts again. "But Bella, this playsuit is so versatile. I can wear it with tights and a cute cardi in the evening or rock it on its own with heels during the day."

"Angel," Bella says in a tone that makes us both aware she is about to pull her older-and-wiser thing again, "neither of you will have ANY – and I repeat, *ANY* – need for heels at this festival. They'll get totally trashed. Right, enough already: I'm going to draw up a list of festival essentials and you two are going to pick ONE holdall each and fill it with only those things, okay?"

Ohmystars, if she's like this now, what's she going to be like at the festival? Or worse still, what's she going to be like as my full-time sister?! I push that thought as far out of my mind as possible and bring myself back to the present, although emptying my holdall of all my pretty things doesn't feel much like a present I really want.

"Look, ladies," Bella says, with slightly less 'tude this time round, "I'm not being the bad dudess here, really I'm not, but not only do I not want your things to get trashed – four Pink Ladies, a Lola mom, my pops and a rucksack each is already going to make for a VERY comfy squeeze in the van too. There's just no way you can take all this, Angel."

Angel pulls a pout that almost matches Bella's in 'tude, but Bella IS older and therefore has had two whole years more practice at it than her. She's also Americano and I think they make them like that there.

No matter how unhappy I am about it, I do not want to ruin my bee-you-tiful pink kitten heels with the big red satin bows, so I be-grudgingly pull out the contents of my bag and spill them onto my bedroom floor. Angel does the same, but not without A LOT of diva-esque huffing and puffing.

"Okay," Bella begins, referring to the list she's been scribbling, "can I get a check on all of the following please?"

Festival Essentials

Underwear, obv. ☐
Wellie boots ☐
Wet wipes ☐
Socks – lots of socks ☐
Towel ☐
Toothbrush and toothpaste ☐
Brush ☐
Sunblock ☐
Jeans ☐
Kicks ☐
Dresses – can be worn over jeans,
or on their own depending on weather ☐
Rain mac ☐
Cardis, jumpers and hoodies ☐
Shades ☐
Camera ☐
Notebook ☐

"What about make-up?" Angel asks, eyeing up her vanity case lovingly. "*And* hair products. Come on, cut me some slack here – I am absolutely going to NEED prodz for this 'fro, dollface!"

"Okay," Bella says, slowly weakening. "You can each have five make-up items and two hair essentials, but that's it!"

"It's like being on that blimmin' reality TV programme that's set in the jungle," Angel moans. "What next? Will I have to eat a kangaroo eye or make eyeliner from a piece of coal?"

"Not a bad idea," Bella says, scratching her chin and pondering that thought. "The coal for kohl, obv, not the eyeball-eating – that's just freakin' gross!".

After about a million years, Angel chooses her prods and lines them up for Bella's approval – plus the three palettes of disco-coloured eyeshadow I've just seen her sneak into her bag while Bella isn't looking.

"Ladies," Bella smiles, giving us both a resounding thumbs-up, "I think we are all good to go; let's hop on board the Bliss bus!"

The Bliss bus?

Angel and I look at each other, exchanging a wide-eyed, psychic, ohmystars-what-on-earth-have-we-let-ourselves-in-for glance and I put on my pink-tinted shades. I have a feeling I'm going to need them.

Chapter Eight

The Road Trip mixtape
Eve and Gwen - Let Me Blow Ya Mind
Blondie - Rapture
Shampoo - Shiny Black Taxi Cab
The Stokes - How Awkward?
Kelk and the Skinny Jeanz - Classy
Elbow - On a Day Like This
Ooh-la-la Aimee - Retro Fabulous
Missy Elliot - Get Ur Freak On
Hole - Doll Parts
Nancy Sinatra - So Long Babe
The Piperita Patties - All My Friends Are Girls

Don't tell anyone, but I'm secretly a little bit excited now. Blondie, an idol-girl in Pink-world, is filling the Bliss bus with 'Rapture', we have yummy eats in the form of Haribo and chocolate buttons, and Miss Sadie, the walking, talking festival cliché in turquoise tights, a tutu that spills from her waist like a frothy strawberry milkshake and sparkly wings, has been collected en route.

"Hey hey festie besties!" she sings, slamming the camper van door behind her and squeezing up next to me. "Look what I've got!"

As she reaches into one of her *two* bags, I can literally hear Angel preparing a childish 'why is Sadie allowed to bring an extra bag and I'm not?' speech in her head, but luckily she stops herself just in time, because Sadie presents each of us with a Pink Lady pink and silver feather boa. She's even making the ma-parental and Yoga Dad wear one. Yep, silliness is now in place; we are officially festival ready.

As much of a fan as I am of road trips, six peeps squished into one camper van is not the stuff pink dreams are made of. Once all the Haribo has gone and we've heard 'Rapture' five times, Sadie suggests a quick round of the classic road trip game 'I went to the shops and I bought...' but in her classic theme-loving way changes it to 'I went to a festival and I took...' It's silly but it's fun and we play at least seven rounds before we get bored. Angel, who is still very bitter at having to leave half of her festival wardrobe on my bedroom floor, starts every round with 'I went to a festival and I took...nothing, because bad Bella said I wasn't allowed.'

"You'll be thanking me when we get there, Angel-face!" Bella insists as she starts to skilfully paint her nails a vamp-girl shade of 'Divinely Dark'.

"Hmm," Angel says, narrowing her eyes, "we'll see."

"Bella!" Yoga Dad calls from the driver seat, "I'm totally impressed at your ability to paint your nails in a moving vehicle but can you at least open a window if you're going to do it?"

Bella rolls her eyes and opens the small back window without smudging a single nail, which, personally, I think is really rather impressive. It's always reassuring to see Bella have a normal reaction to a parental instruction. She and Yoga Dad are usually so chilled out in each other's company, it freaks me out.

I take a look at the back of the ma-parental's head and even though I can't see her face, I know that she's smiling. It feels so weird to think that a year ago, if I'd even suggested the idea of going to a festival (which I know is unthinkable, but please...go with me on this one) she would've absolutely, positively said 'No way, Lola love, not a chance, nope, nada,' and if I'd mentioned the possibility that she come too? Well, I think she would've certified me seven kinds of crazy. Yet here we both are, avec three Pink Ladies and a Yoga Dad, in a camper van, making our way to a festival, singing at the top of our voices to my most favourite MySpace find, The Piperita Patties. In all the pages of my journal, where I create scenes and magic moments for my movie, *Livin' La Vida Lola*, I don't think I'd ever have been able to dream up *this* particular scenario.

"Ladies," Yoga Dad declares after what feels like a lifetime, "we're here!"

Sadie lets out a trademark Sadie-squeal of excitement as Yoga Dad rolls down his window and flashes a pass at a bearded man in a fluorescent jacket.

"Hi there sir," the fluoro-man says, checking the pass carefully, "will you be requiring the VIP parking area?"

"No, thank you," Yoga Dad says politely, "we've got passes to camp."

"Oh," says fluoro-man looking confused, "it's just that this pass gives you unlimited access to the entire backstage area, sir."

"Oh, I know," Yoga Dad says in his positive and breezy style, "but how are we to have a true festival experience if we're not camping out with everyone else?"

The fluoro-man shrugs his shoulders and points us in the direction of a long stream of cars making their way to a field with tents in it.

"Um..." I begin, in a state of 'woah-there' shock and horror, "I think you're right, y'know: all that listening to my iPod *must* have made my ears go funny, because I thought I just heard you turn down 'Access All Areas' so that we can camp in a muddy field with no access to running water instead..."

"Of course not, Lola," Yoga Dad says cheerily, as he negotiates the lumps and bumps in the field.

"Ohmystars, thank goodness for that!" I say, breathing a huge sigh of relief.

"No – it hasn't rained in days so it's not muddy at all, and there's definitely running water, because they have showers..."

If I didn't know better, I'd think he was being sarcastic, but what with him being a) Yoga Dad and b) an Americano and all, I know this isn't something he knows an awful lot about.

"But seriously," I say, aware of the slightly whiney sound that I'm making and am doing nothing to stop, "if we're allowed to camp backstage, what with you being a yoga-dude to the stars and everything, why are we camping here, exactly?"

"Because Pops wants us to have a real festival experience," Bella interrupts, shaking her head, "right, Pops?"

"Exactly," Yoga Dad agrees, as he comes to a sudden stop next to a group of boys attempting to put up their tent.

Angel, having spotted this potential new festival highlight, taps my arm and whispers, "it might just be okay, Lo-Lo!"

"Okay girls," Yoga Dad continues, unbuckling his seat belt, jumping out the van and running around to open the side door, "out you get – the Bliss Weekender starts here!"

Chapter Nine

Sadie, who is acting like an excited pup about to be taken on the best walk *ever*, jumps out first, followed swiftly by Bella. She pinches Sadie's shoulders as they jibber-jabber about their list of must-see bands. Angel and I are lacking the enthusiasm of our fellow pink counterparts due to long-term minibus squishage and we shake our heads in complete bemusement.

Does Yoga Dad not realise that Angel and I might not want a real festival experience when there's backstage luxury on offer? In fact, I thought we'd made it really, really clear that we'd do anything NOT to have a real festival experience? Apparently, it seems Yoga Dad, in his infinite yoga-like wisdom, has chosen to ignore that particular memo.

I push my pink-tinted shades up my nose, wanting to take them back and ask for a refund, because no matter how pink-tinted my world is through these lenses, I'm struggling to find anything particularly pink and positive right now. I've tried to be all psyched about the whole tent situ but now I'm here, it's a struggle. Especially now I know I'm going to be camping in a field when I could have been living the life with an Access All Areas pass to the celebrity luxe, sipping pink lemonade and eating strawberries dipped in chocolate after enjoying a really nice shower that I haven't had to share with a million gazillion other people.

What's that? I'm a diva?

Possibly.

"Smell that fresh air!" Bella says, pulling up her neon green knee-high socks and doing a twirl in the pale yellow petticoat that she's wearing as a skirt. "Isn't it amazing?"

Angel is shaking her head in total disbelief.

I remind her that *she* was the one who talked me into this whole festival fiasco. "It'll be fun, Lola – c'mon!' she said. Hmmph! Who's laughing now, Miss Angel Trueman?

"Bella," Angel says matter-of-factly, putting her hands on her hips, "this air is *not* fresh. It's normal air with the smell of cow poop in it; that's not fresh, that's just wrong."

I snigger at Angel, her glam-girl self, looking as out of place in this field as a goth-girl would at Disneyland.

"Look," Sadie says, pulling out the pink leopard-print tent from the van, and throwing it to the floor with a thud, "will you two just pack it in with your townie 'tude? Bella and I wanted to come last night so we could get the full festie experience, but Yoga Dad said that we should just leave early this morning instead so that you only had to have two nights in the great outdoors, so think yourself lucky! We are going to be happy campers and it's going to be fun. You remember that, don't you? Y'know, *fun*? It's what Pink Ladies do, except you wouldn't know it, because two particular Pink Ladies seem to have forgotten how!"

Angel and I exchange a glance. Yep, we've just been well and truly Sadied. Things have to be really bad for her to stamp her pixie-sized foot. I feel a pang of guilt the size of Scotland for making this experience all about me. It's obvious that Bella and Sadie are super-excited and if the idea of not going to toilet for two days – believe me, I'm going to try not to – isn't bothering them, then it really shouldn't be bothering me, either. I AM being a diva, and not the Think Pink kind but the foot-stomping, hissy-fit throwing kind

– and that kind are very un-pretty.

"Hey Angel," I say, trying desperately to find a way to show Miss Sadie that Angel and I really can do this, "do you remember when we were small and we persuaded your totally bewildered parentals to let us sleep in your back garden?"

Angel raises her eyes to the sky, trying to recall the memory from the filing cabinet in her mind, but it must be nestled deep between thoughts of sky-high killer heels and beyond-expensive designer handbags. After several seconds of vacant, a look of recognition returns to her flawless face.

"In my Barbie tent!" she shouts. "OMG, I remember!"

"Wasn't it fun? Sleeping under the stars?" I smile, remembering how excited and scared we were when we looked outside the tent to see that the moon and the stars were our ceiling for the night. "And eating marshmallows until we felt sick!"

"I *was* sick!" Angel screams with laughter. "I stuck my head outside the tent and just threw up! Mum said we should sleep inside because we couldn't sleep where I'd just been sick, but we cried and cried until finally Dad came out and moved the tent."

"You were both divas even then!" Bella shakes her head but at least everyone is smiling again. Angel puts her thumb to her nose and waggles her fingers at her, and in return Bella blows a raspberry.

"Okay then," Sadie says, the excitement making her voice rise an entire octave, "if it helps, let's think of this as a slumber party *sur l'herbe*. We've got our best buds, tiny travel games, a guitar – because sleeping in a tent just isn't be the same without a campfire sing-song – and a Frisbee for between-band summer fun, 'k?"

Sadie has this real knack of being able to make what might not be totally what you want to do suddenly become the best idea in the world, ever – I love her for that.

"And..." Bella says, rummaging around in her backpack, "I've brought along some beauty samples for everyone, which will come in handy what with the showers being less than spa-like."

"Bella, I could kiss you!" Angel screams, performing a mini knee slide as she dives to get her hands on the sweet-smelling treats.

"Angel," Bella says, tapping her hand away and zipping her bag back up, "they're for later. Seriously, there's no reason why The Great Outdoors and glamour should be mutually exclusive, y'know. F'sure, nylon ground sheets might not be a glamorous essential but we can still make the tent totally gorgeous. Once it's all set up, we'll throw these in." Bella pulls out a bin liner filled with cosy cushions and silky quilts. Now this is more like it: we're going to create our own outdoor luxe, Pink Lady style.

"Girls, before you get started," Yoga Dad interrupts, "if it's okay with you, we're just going to go meet with the organisers and see where I'm needed."

Yoga Dad has magically transformed from camper-van-driving hippy to head-to-toe yoga guru in the blink of an eye. His traditional all-white kundalini outfit – white linen trousers, linen kaftan and white turban to cover his hair – looks simply serene amongst all the noise and craziness. No wonder those celeb-types pay crazy money to get bendy with him. Mum is looking at him in complete adoration and it's like she's forgotten that there's anyone else here, including me.

"Mum," I ask, making an effort to include her in Pink Lady activities, "did you want to stay here and help us set up?"

"Thanks, Lola," she says, not looking away from Yoga Dad, "but I'm going to go watch the guru in action – are you okay?"

"Of course she's okay," Bella says, putting her arm around my shoulder. "Lola just needed a little bit of gentle persuasion that this was a neat idea? Right?"

"Right," I say, giving both Bella and The Mothership as big a smile as I can manage. I'm not sure I need Bella to tell me what to say to my own mother, but I don't want to cause a fuss, I just want to put the tent up so I know I've at least got somewhere to sleep.

"You're coming back, aren't you?" Bella asks The Mothership, "It's just that before we go to see Ooh-la-la Aimee, I want to take you to this really amazing holistic SHA wellness place in the healing field that you'll just love!"

"Of course, I'll look forward to it, Bella," The Mothership coos. I'm not sure she even knows what holistic SHA wellness is, but who knows? Bella seems to know her a whole lot better than me these days.

"Oh and girls, before I go," Yoga Dad says, "I want you to meet my friends Hamish and Loretta, their son, Alwyn and his friends. They're responsible for saving us a good spot!"

The boys, who Angel was checking out earlier, all turn around to give us a wave, and we politely wave back, secretly scoping them out for their potential crushability factor. Come on, it would be rude not to, right?

"If you girls need a hand," shouts Hamish, the big dude with long dark hair and a huge bush-like beard, "these boys will be only too happy to help!"

They groan and we laugh and when Yoga Dad is happy that we're happy, he and the ma-parental make their own happy by holding hands as they walk down towards the main event. I look away. Grown-up mush-stuff makes me feel a little bit Icksville.

Chapter Ten

Potential our-age mush-stuff, on the other hand, well...that makes me positively coo with sweetness, especially when it involves Miss Sadie and a boy with blue stripes across his cheeks, wearing a band of brown suede around his head, Rambo-style, with a single red and green feather in it.

"Hey!" he says, raising a hand and locking eyes with Pink Lady, Sadie. Sadie blushes bright red and looks away. Ooh, boy crushage would be a very new development in Sadie-World.

"How now, brown cow!" Bella replies, before making a 'woah-woah-woah' noise by tapping her hand against her mouth.

"Ahh, Bella," the feather-wearing boy replies, "how I've missed your comic ways."

"I'm sure you have, son of Bearded One," Bella says, ruffling the boy's hair. "Now come here and give me a hug!"

"Do I have to?" he pleads, putting his hands together in a prayer-like way.

"Yes, you have to!" Bella says, wrapping her long arms around him. "Everyone!" Bella announces, hanging her arm around feather-boy like a new line in off-the-shoulder accessories, "this is Alwyn, son of The Bearded One!"

Hamish, the big dude with the hair and the beard lets out a big hefty laugh that could only belong to a man that big.

"He's a boy scout you know," Bella continues, purposely trying to embarrass him, "so what he doesn't know about putting up tents just isn't worth knowing, right kid?!"

"Bella!" Alwyn says, brushing off Bella's arm, and trying to meet Sadie's eyes. "I *was* a boy scout; I'm not anymore – and I'm not a kid either... I mean, hello? I'm fourteen years old!"

"That's why you're wearing that super-mature ensemble, is it?" Bella sniggers. "Because you're not a kid?"

"Duh. It's a theme, Bella, can't you tell?" he says, pointing to his friends who are opening cans of Coke and admiring their finished put-up-tent masterpiece. "We've come as characters from old Western movies. I'm Big Chief Blue Face, and the boys, well, they're a various assortment of wannabe cowboys!"

"Howdy!" one of the boys shouts, lifting his hat from his head in comedy cowboy fashion.

"I was a Brownie," Sadie squeaks, as if trying to save Alwyn from anymore Bella-like grief. "Maybe between us we could do this before it starts to get dark? It's just that I have a sneaky suspicion that these two here have NO idea how to put up a tent!"

By 'these two', Sadie is clearly referring to Angel and I, and of course her assumptions are correct. That whole Barbie tent/camping in the garden thing was a LONG time ago.

"We can read instructions, y'know!" I protest – not too much though, as I get the feeling Sadie would rather like Big Chief Blue Face to earn his Sadie-designed 'I can put up a tent' badge by helping her.

"A Brownie?" Alwyn says, a toothy smile filling his entire face at the idea of helping Sadie. "That's cool!"

He kneels down beside her and pulls out a pole and some tent pegs. The two of them look like real-life cartoon characters, her in her fairy wings and him with a feather in his hair; all that's missing is cartoon hearts in hot pink popping above their heads.

As much as I really would help to put up the tent, I don't want to disturb the potential love-mush, so I pull out my journal and start taking notes.

The thing about journal writing, especially in a public setting, is that it heightens your hearing. I'm not sure if that's like a scientific fact or whatever, but it's a Lola fact and they're by far my most favourite kind. Anyway, so while I'm taking notes about the road trip, making a potential playlist to put in the next edition of my zine and making a quick sketch of the cuteness that is Alwyn and Sadie, I tune into conversations without people actually knowing I'm doing it – cool, huh?! It's like a superpower or something.

Except as soon as I start, I realise right away that I absolutely shouldn't, because Bella is talking to The Bearded One and his wife about Yoga Dad. And the ma-parental.

"Loretta, she's just perfect for dad," Bella tells The Bearded One's wife. "I think it was fate that we moved next door to her and Lola. And I expect dad's fully signed-up membership to the karma club had something to do with it too!"

The three of them laugh and Bella takes a swig from her bottle of water.

"So when did they get together?" Loretta asks.

"I think they secretly liked each other straight away," Bella says, before lowering her voice a little bit, "except when we arrived, Lola's dad had just left and Lola and her mom weren't exactly BFFs, which I just don't get, because her mom is awesome. So anyway, they've been keeping things on the down-low because Lola's still a bit...y'know, about her dad leaving, but have you ever seen my dad so happy?"

"No," says Loretta, turning to Hamish, "we were just saying that, weren't we Hamish? He gives so much to others, with his kindness and the work that he does, we always thought it was such a shame that he hadn't found someone special...y'know, after..."

"I know," Bella's voice cracks a little bit. There's a pause in the conversation so I look up to see Bella and Loretta exchanging a hug.

Well, that was an insight into my own life I wasn't expecting.

I turn to Angel to see if she was able to perfect the same convo-dropping skills whilst applying make-up, but it seems that prettification is all-encompassing, because she's positively oblivious as she paints little pink stars in the corner of each eye with pink sparkly eyeliner.

I quickly scribble in my journal what I'm feeling, which is confusion and a big, fat bunch of weird. Have the ma-parental and Yoga Dad really been into each other for such a long time? And if that *is* the case then surely I would have noticed? And I am trying really hard not to get all kinds of mad with Bella for making judgments about my relationship with The Mothership but I can't quite seem to fight it. She doesn't know what The Mothership was like when dad left – in fact, there's a lot Bella doesn't know. And what happened to Yoga Dad that made Bella make eye-water? Under normal circumstances, I'd channel my inner detective girl, who, btw, has nothing on that Nancy Drew, but because of the big, fat bunch of weird that I'm feeling, I just store my thoughts in my journal and slam it shut tight.

Chapter Eleven

"Alwyn!" Cowboy One calls, although, if I'm honest, he looks more like Woody from *Toy Story* than a cowboy from the black and white Westerns. "We're going down to the main arena – we really want to catch Do You Want A Kipper Before You Leave, Kelly?. You coming, Big Chief?"

I saw Do You Want A Kipper Before You Leave, Kelly? on some TV programme a week ago. They wore capes and spoke in some crazy Victoriana-style language and, while I giggled at the time, I'm pretty sure the novelty will soon wear off. I'm not really in a wacky comedy place, after all, so I stay schtum.

"Thanks boys," he says, hitting the last tent post in place with a big mallet, "but no, you go ahead. When I'm finished up here, I'm going to head over to the drumming workshop – don't forget to saddle up your horses before you go!"

His pals laugh, pull on their wristbands and wave goodbye.

"You play drums?" Sadie asks him as they both stand back to admire their handiwork.

"I do; I play in a band with those guys – we're called Vote Pedro, y'know, after *Napoleon Dynamite*?" he says, putting his hand to his eyes to shade them from the sun.

"No way!" Sadie squeals, almost doing on-the-spot star jumps.

"I play drums too, and we've got a band – we're called The Rainbow Hearts because...well, that's what Bella named us – and I LOVE *Napoleon Dynamite*, it's one of my favourite films!"

These cutesters are absolutely, positively cute-ing me out.

"Really?" Alwyn says. "Well, did you want to come to the drumming workshop with me? It's all bongo beats and African rhythms – it's going to be ace!"

Sadie looks at Bella, who has made a crazy-detailed plan of all the bands and places that we're all going to see, but Bella, who has now wiped away the eye-water and has taken off her biker boots to get some sun on her legs – she is a Cali-girl, after all, and they love the sun – shoos her away.

"It's fine, Sadiecakes," Bella says in a pretend 'I'm-put-out' voice, "I see what's happened here: you've made a new friend and now you're blowing out your old ones!"

Sadie doesn't see Bella secretly wink at Alwyn and gets into an insta-fluster at the thought of upsetting her BFF.

"That's not true," Sadie protests, "it's just I've always wanted to play the bongos, you know that!"

"Hmmm..." Bella says, not making eye contact with Sadie. I might still be a little mad at Bella but she does make me giggle. "Maybe..."

"You know I have, Bella!" Sadie says, turning red.

"Take no notice of her," Alwyn says, touching her arm. "She's teasing you, Sadie!"

Bella lets out a whoop, and Sadie digs her in the shoulder with her finger.

"Ouch!" Bella screams, rubbing at her just-been-prodded shoulder. "Just don't blame me if you miss Ooh-la-la Aimee, that's all. Yoga Dad said he's going to ring me when he's finished his session so we can go meet her!"

"It's okay, Bells," Sadie says, rubbing her hands with excitement. "You know I'd like to meet her, but c'mon, she's your thing isn't she? And drums...well, they're *my* thing. And we'll all go see The Tootie tomorrow, right?"

"Right!" I say, jumping to my feet and giving her a hug. "Have fun, awesome girl."

"Yep," Sadie says, turning to Alwyn, "I'm sure we will!"

"Cool!" he says, grabbing a set of old-looking bongo drums from his tent. "Then we'd better get going – it's in the red area and it might take us a little while to get there. You ready?"

"Ready!" Sadie shouts, as she grabs her Hello Kitty rucksack, puts it in on the front way round so that she doesn't crush her wings, and flashes him a smile. He flashes one right back, although seriously, his face must be one big ache because he has been smiling ever since he set eyes on Sadie.

"Thanks for putting the tent up, guys!" I call after them as they skip into the distance like they're in some kind of fairytale adventure.

"No worries!" Alwyn replies, throwing an arm in the air by way of recognition.

"How adorbs are those two?" I ask, watching their silhouettes become teeny, tiny specks on the horizon.

"Yep," Angel confirms, "it's official: cute just got out-cuted!"

"I know," Bella agrees, pulling all the pretty cushions that she's brought with us out of the carrier bag, "they're literally boy-girl versions of each other, aren't they? I so should have thought about hooking them up before."

Bella throws a fuchsia pink cushion at Angel, and a turquoise one at me. "So, now they've done the hard bit," Bella says, as she climbs inside our pink leopard-print Casa Bliss, "we get to do the fun part: making it pretty!"

Angel and I follow Bella into the tent and spend half an hour pulling out cushions, hanging sparkly bunting, laying out our glam-girl sleeping bags and covering them with coloured blankets, until finally, it becomes less four person tent and more boutique-style hotel.

"Nice job, ladies," I say, holding both hands up for a double high five. "This camping lark might just turn out to be okay after all."

"Sorry Lo," Bella coughs, cocking her head to one side and placing her hand to her ear. "Sorry, I didn't quite catch that?"

Chapter Tweleve

The sound of Bella's ringtone – Blondie's 'Call Me' – fills our tent, but Bella doesn't answer it until the very last minute so that the three of us can sing 'Call Me!' at the top of our voices and do an upper body wiggle in time to the tune. It's like a Pink Lady ritual.

"Hola!" Bella shouts, catching the caller just before Blondie sends him to the answer machine.

"Hey Pops...5pm? Awesome... Where?" Bella grips her mobile between her shoulder and her ear, bites the lid off a pen, and uses the palm of her hand as a notepad. "Okay, cool... Pops, you rock...thank you! Okay, I'll see you then... Peace, out!"

"Peace, out?" I say, confused at Bella's new '80s style sign-off.

"Lo-Lo, please don't ruin my post-call buzz," Bella pouts, slipping her phone back in her bag and clapping her hands with excitement. "So guess what? We're meeting her by the Electro stage, wherever that is, and Pops has been asked to give her a pre-set yoga session – how awesome is that? What if he becomes her personal yoga-teacher?! We'd become friends and she'd ask me to play guitar on her next record and we'd tour the country—"

"Whoa there, Bells," Angel says, holding her hands up in

surrender, "you're literally bombarding my ears with word noise... Please pause, now rewind. Who are we seeing? What time? And *when* are you going on tour with her?"

"Jeez..." Bella sighs, almost exhausted by our inability to keep up with her new Sadie-speed excitement. "I'm not going on tour with her – not yet, anyway – but maybe once I've met her I can persuade her!"

"Jeez Louise..." Angel huffs, shifting herself to her knees. "Who are you talking about?!"

"Ooh-la-la Aimee, of course!" Bella shouts.

"Ohhh," Angel says, returning to her cross-legged position. "I know her. There was loads of controversy between her and *Fierce* magazine – they were going to do a massive breakthrough artist type feature and her people said she'd only do it if she got cover, and apparently Skye Summers – y'know her, Lo, the editor – she said only *she* decides who goes on the cover, not the artist!"

"But Skye's not like that," I protest, because I do know her. She's my Aunt Lullah's best friend and having stayed with her in Londonium earlier in the year while I did work experience at *Missy* mag, I just know she wouldn't say something like that. "Where did you hear that?"

"It was on all the fash pack blogs, Lola," Angel sighs. "Anyway, so we're going to meet her? This Ooh-la-la Aimee? Cool! When?"

"At five," Bella says, tapping a non-existent watch on her bracelet-filled arm, "so we should start getting ready really. I was thinking hot pink lips, big purple bow in my hair and yellow and pink sun-dress with the black boots, obv..."

"Bells," Angel says, "while I applaud your fashion sense – you know it's one of the many things I love about you – it's just that the Vivienne Sui fashion show starts at five, and it's kinda the whole reason that I've come..."

"Oh, no way!" Bella pouts. "I really wanted to see the fashion show too – Vivienne Sui is awesome. But there is no way I'm going to turn down face time with Aimee; that would just be freakin' crazy!"

"Of course!" Angel nods, putting together her own ensemble of black lacy leggings, silver sequined hot pants with yellow trim, a black vest and a matching sequined waistcoat. "So, what are you going to do, Lola – go meet Aimee or head to the fashion show with me?"

Oh.

I hadn't counted on having to choose between the fashion show and meeting this amazing Miss Ooh-la-la Aimee. This isn't fair. Okay, so when in doubt, I always find it useful to call upon one of three silver screen goddesses: Audrey Hepburn, Marilyn Monroe or Jane Mansfield. I'm aware that none of the above would ever choose to be at a festival but if, like me, they found themselves in this sorry situation, what would they do? Today I choose Marilyn.

What would Marilyn do?

Marilyn would go to the fashion show, I just know it. Besides, I'm not that into Ooh-la-la Aimee. F'sure, the girl knows how to rock an outfit, but I don't know whether I particularly want to meet her, especially if her and her 'people' are bad-mouthing Skye. That is not cool with me. And I'm not desperate to spend any alone time with Bella just yet.

"It's completely up to you, Lo," Bella says as she wriggles out of her denim shorts and pulls her yellow sundress over her hips. "It's just, I thought it might be cool if, before we met Aimee, we scooped your mom up from Pop's workshop and took her to the holistic SHA healing place together."

"Oh yeah?" I say, busying myself with choosing my own outfit and popping a marshmallow in my mouth to avoid actually having to speak. Hmm, probably not ready for Bella/Lola/Mothership time.

"Yeah, then I thought we could all go get a henna tattoo from Kandy, this really cool girl I know; she's here every year. I thought it would be, like, a really cool family-girl-bonding thing to do. So what do you think?"

Now *that* I am definitely not ready for. If Marilyn and I hadn't already made my decision, then I deffo would have been able to based on the whole 'cool family-girl-bonding thing'.

"That sounds really great, Bells," I say, searching for the right words to use. "It's just, I'd kind of promised Angel I'd go to the fashion show with her already, didn't I, Angel?"

"You did?" Angel asks, looking at me with an 'oh-no-you-didn't' face. As Bella pulls her green hoodie over her head, I squeeze Angel's arm tight and scowl at her. "Oh yeah, that's right, yes you did!"

"Never mind," Bella says, pulling the hoodie back off and tying it around her waist instead, "not to worry, more face time for me to persuade her that she needs me in her band!"

"We could meet up after?" I say, trying to save my place in the karma club. "Maybe you could call us when you're done and we could catch some music together?"

"Sure thing," Bella calls back as she crawls out the tent. "I'm off to explore – you two kids have a fun time at the fashion show."

"We will!" Angel calls after her. "Give our love to Aimee – take pictures!"

"Will do," Bella says, poking her head back in through the tent flaps. "Peace out."

"Okay, Lola Love," Angel says, folding her arms. "Care to tell me what all that was about?"

Chapter Thirteen

Having now changed into my own festie outfit – a simple white vest with an oversized pink bow attached, a pink rah-rah skirt, a pink beret and my oversized pink-tinted shades – Angel and I zip up the pink leopard-print door to Casa Bliss, padlock it shut, leave the keys with Hamish and Loretta, and make our way to the main event.

"So now are you going to explain, Lola?" Angel asks, pulling her ridiculously huge bright yellow sunhat down as far as it'll go over her big-as-a-house afro.

"There's nothing *to* explain," I say, trying to loosen the super-tight ponytail Bella has pulled my pink tresses into. "I just didn't want Bella to think I was choosing you over her, that's all."

"Hmmm," Angel says. "Something tells me you're not being a hundred per cent honest with me, Lola Love. Do I sense that those Gloomy Grumps aren't quite gone yet?"

"I am," I say, linking arms with Angel, whose sequins are literally blinding people as we walk past them, "really, I am! Now come on, let's go do this festival thing!"

"Hmmm..." she says again, but this time it's not at me, it's at a group of boys in various states of undress. Why is it that, at the slightest hint of sun, British boys think that it's really okay to walk around without any upper body garments? Right now though, I'm not going to question it, because any distraction is a welcome distraction.

I mean, I just don't know what to say. I can't say I'm jealous of Bella doing things with The Mothership if I'm not prepared to go hang with them both, can I? And I can't say that I don't want Yoga Dad and the ma-parental to get together when The Mothership is quite clearly the happiest she's ever been, can I?

"Thing is, Lola," Angel begins, as we pass the bare-chested boys of summer, "it's all very well those boys showing bare flesh, and while my head may have been turned momentarily, nothing – I repeat, *nothing* – will stand between me and the fashion. Get me to the show, pronto!"

I love Angel Trueman.
Superficial? Yes.
Adorable with it? Abso-blimmin'-lutely.

The festival site is mesmerizing. We've literally passed a million, gazillion tents to get to the main gate and while there *are* a few silly types without tops or sun-block (they'll be sorry in the morning) and a few people with dreadlocks and big velvet jester hats with bells on, Bella's right: the main festival uniform is pretty dresses and wellie boots for the girls and jeans and t-shirts for the boys, which may be why, when Angel and I pass through the main gate and into the throng of people, we become quite the spectacle.

"Why's everyone staring?" Angel asks, tilting her hat a little to the left. She says it like it's a bad thing, but when you've known Angel Trueman as long as I have, you know that if people weren't staring at her, there'd be trouble.

"Um," I begin, "maybe because, in that hat, you look like you're channelling Joan Collins on holiday in the South of France?"

"Do you think?" Angel ponders, really rather pleased with the comparison. "It wasn't the actual look I was going for, but, y'know, Joan was a style icon!"

Joan Collins was, and still is, a super-glam British actress who was in this awesome bitch-fest eighties show called *Dynasty* but now writes slightly rude books about glitzy-glam fabulousness in Hollywood. I only know this because Aunt Lullah always says that reading Joan's books is like her guilty pleasure: she'd never read them in public, but if it was raining outside, she would stay under her duvet and get lost in a Joan Collins book.

"It's not like it matters anyway, is it?" I remind her, while looking for a sign to point us in the direction of the fashion tent. "It's much better to stand out than blend in!"

"Exactly!" she says, waving at a group of boys biting into grease-laden burgers. "We are stars, Lola Love – it would simply be rude not to shine!"

She takes my hand and we trot on like we're joint first prize winners in a gymkhana. Seriously, the only place we belong is the fashion tent. Well, it would be, if only we knew where it was. After walking for what feels like a hundred years, the smell of fried onions laced with sweet candyfloss assaulting my taste buds, I am more than willing to let a big juicy cheeseburger come between me and fashion.

Angel, however, is not.

"There it is!" she screams, as if she has just discovered Marc Jacobs is having a half price sale on handbags. "There's the fashion tent – finally! Come on Lola!"

I take one last long lingering look at the burgers before running to catch up with Angel who is already at the door of the pink and white candy-striped tent of fashion.

"What do you mean, we can't come in?" Angel is saying to the tall, thin girl holding a clipboard.

Uh oh.

"You have to have a ticket or be on the list," the girl pouts, clearly enjoying her position of power. "Do you have a ticket?"

"Well, no," Angel says, with her signature Angel 'tude, "I wasn't aware that I needed one. So where do I get one from?"

"You can't just *get* one," Tall Thin Girl laughs, tapping her pen on her clipboard. "We've sold out – and I'm guessing by the look on your face that you're not on the list?"

"Well, no," Angel repeats, in a tone that I know I wouldn't mess with. "No, clearly we're not."

"Well then," Tall Thin Girl says with a smirk, "I'm afraid you're not coming in."

But what Tall Thin Girl hasn't reckoned on is Angel's ability to always get what she wants.

"Who does she think she is, Lo-Lo?" Angel's voice has gone practically ultrasonic as we make our way to the side of the tent. "She was smirking at me, did you see? She was *actually smirking.*"

It's clear that no amount of foot-stomping and hissy-fit throwing is going to get Angel what she wants, but Pink Thinking? Well, Pink Thinking just might.

"Um, Angel," I say, stretching my neck across the barrier for a better look, "isn't that the fashion guy you met the other day at Rumble in the Jumble?"

Angel follows my finger to see the flamboyant and totally over-the-top Chris Huang flouncing his way through the crowd.

"OMG!" she squeals, her frown instantly turning upside down, "yes, yes it is, Lola!

"Darling!" she coos, sashaying her way to the barrier. "Hey Chris, it's me, Angel!"

It's clear from the expression on his face that he has no recognition at all of who she is, but Angel is completely undeterred by this minor technicality, and beckons him over.

"Chris," she says, pulling him close to kiss the air on both sides of his cheek, "how you doing? You're looking fabulous, by the way... So, can you believe that Lola and I have forgotten our tickets?"

"Oh, no way," Chris says, desperately searching for clues as to who this well-dressed glam-girl actually is.

"I know!" Angel declares. "Crazy! So, do you think you could be a total doll and speak to whoever you need to speak to, to sort this minor misunderstanding out?!"

Angel's 'we're-total-be-there-buds' act works surprisingly well, because even though he doesn't have a clue who we are, he's in fashion, sweetie, and with Angel dressed like a total Glamazon, he'd be all sorts of rude and wrong NOT to get her in.

So he does.

I know.

Angel can't resist blowing Tall Thin Girl a cheeky kiss as Chris flashes his pass and all three of us saunter past.

"Ladies," Chris says, pointing towards two spare seats near the back, "that's all I'm going to be able to manage, I'm afraid – the show's about to start!"

"Thank you so much, Chris," Angel says, taking her seat. I take my seat next to her and shake my head in disbelief.

"Angel Trueman," I say, "you're unbelievable, do you know that?!"

"I do – but so are you, Lo-Lo," Angel smiles, making herself comfy on the flip chairs. "If you hadn't seen Chris, we'd still be outside – teamwork!"

We do a mini high five, keeping it down low so as not to draw too much attention to our non-ticket-holding selves.

"So okay, it's not front row," Angel says as she surveys the marquee, "but hey, at least we're in... Now, let the show begin!"

Within seconds, Angel is in complete fashion heaven, pointing out designers and celeb-types in the crowd and on the catwalk. The show itself is spectacular. Kelk and The Skinny Jeanz, today's headlining act, are providing the music as crazy-beautiful models, including The Piperita Patties and Jodie from The Heike/Cross Love Project show off Vivienne Sui's latest collection. Hot pink scarves worn as an obi belt, tattoo-print tops in flesh colours: v.cool; denim romper suits worn with mad-sized heels: crazy.

If I wrote for one of those swanky fash mags, I'd say it's a geisha and rockabilly inspired mix-up that makes a surprisingly audacious fashion moment. So there.

"Wow!" I shout as the lights go up. "That was incredible, wasn't it?"

"You're telling me, Lola!" Angel claps. "Aaa-mazing – nice work Chris! Except can you believe he actually didn't remember me? These fashion types Lo – so shallow!"

"Hey, Lola," a voice from behind me shouts above the hustle

and bustle of the fash pack, "is that you?"

"Skye!" I shout, reaching out to envelop the most glamorous Glamazonian in Glamazonia in a Lola hug. "What are you doing here?"

"I could ask you the same thing!" Skye says, waving at someone who looks suspiciously like Jimmy from The Hotsters – FYI, he is indeed hot. Very. "Do you know how hard it was to get tickets for this thing?!"

Angel and I exchange a cheeky glance.

"Skye Summers," I say, as I take the hand of my BFF, Angel, "I'd like you to meet Angel Trueman, the proud owner of your posh shoes with the red soles! Angel Trueman, meet Skye Summers, Aunt Lullah's best friend and editor-in-chief at *Fierce* magazine."

"Ahh, so you're the fashionista!" Skye says, holding her hand out to shake Angel's. "As I can see."

"I am, I am," Angel gushes. "Thank you so much for the heels, they're increds. It's such a treat to meet you, Skye – I love the magazine. Is it true you wouldn't put Ooh-la-la Aimee on the cover?"

Skye shoots me a 'get-me-out-of-here' look, but luckily my diversion skills are not required due to the arrival of Chris Huang, who, having seen Angel talking to Skye Summers, has realised she must be a pretty cool person to know after all.

"So ladies, did you enjoy the show?" Chris says, linking his arm with Angel's. We all nod, but Chris is looking mainly at Skye, what with her being such a big name in the fashion world and everything.

"So would you like to come backstage and meet Vivienne?" he asks, holding out three passes.

"I would!" Angel says, practically snatching the pass from his hand and giving me a 'could this day get any better?' look.

"Thanks for the offer," Skye says, "but I'm having lunch with her on Monday. And I'm starving. I don't suppose you fancy joining me for a slice of cake and a glass of lemonade, girls?"

"Angel, do you mind?" I ask, giving her my best puppy-dog

impression. If seeing Skye wasn't temptation enough, she just used the magical 'C' word. Cake.

"Of course not, gorgeous girl, but you don't mind if I go do you?" Angel smiles, tightening her grip on her backstage pass. "Chris here will look after me, won't you Chris?"

"Absolutely!" Chris says. "Let's go and be fabulous, sweetie!"

Angel gives me a l'il wink before skipping off into the fashionista crowd.

"So, this offer of cake and lemonade," I quiz Skye, "does it extend to the use of a clean toilet?"

"Of course it does!" Skye laughs. "I have press passes!"

Backstage luxe in the form of cold lemonade, cake and access to clean toilets?

"Then count me in!"

Chapter Fourteen

Skye reaches into her blood red, beyond expensive patent handbag and hands me a blue wristband. Okay, so it's not an Access All Areas laminated pass, but it's deffo better than your average festival-goer green band. I stretch it over my hand and feel like a proper journo-girl as I head backstage with Skye.

It seems as busy back here as it is out front, but everyone looks a little bit...y'know, cleaner. I follow Skye's lead as she picks up a paper plate and loads it up with a handful of grapes and a jumbo slice of cheesecake. I too take a handful of grapes, but I choose a jumbo portion of chocolate cake that is basically screaming, 'Lola, you must eat me, it's the law!'

"So where's the till?" I ask, filling a plastic cup with lemonade from the machine.

"You don't have to pay, silly!" Skye laughs, picking up a bar of chocolate and slipping it into her bag. "It's free! Why do you think so many people try to blag their way backstage? You wouldn't stay out there if you had access to this, would you?"

I slip a bar of chocolate into my bag too, because free chocolate is the very best chocolate.

"Well, you would if you were the guy that my ma-parental is seeing," I tell Skye, as we take a seat in the shade under a parasol decorated with teeny tiny hanging pieces of reflective mirrors – very Moroccan-chic. "He's a yoga-guru type dude and all the stars use him, except he has us all camping in a field, a million miles away, so that we can get a 'real' festival experience!"

"Ahhh, the yoga dude..." Skye says between mouthfuls. "Your aunt Lullah mentioned him. So what do you think, then? Is he cool?"

"Yeah, he's a cool guy," I say, taking a good sigh. "It could definitely be worse."

But if it could be worse than why do I STILL feel the big fat bunch of weird anytime anyone mentions it?

"I think Lullah's just pleased your mum's happy," Skye says, resting her fork on the side of her plate and stretching her long legs out in the sun.

"Yeah, I am too," I say, and change the subject really quickly because, seriously, I'm backstage eating chocolate cake with Skye Summers: this is no time for glum-girl thoughts. "So, did you have fun with Lullah in New York?" I ask, popping a grape in my mouth.

"Oh Lola," Skye says, visibly melting into a moment-o of happiness, "it was a blast! I'm so glad I went. And I'm so proud of her – you have to go visit her, Lola; her apartment is amazing! It's in Brooklyn, where all the cool slinkster people hang out, and we did some dancing at the Bowery Ballroom to some impossibly cool bands – best times. Oh, and she was totally jealous that I got hang-time with you when you were in London; she misses you so much, y'know!"

I miss her too. Very much. Aunt Lullah was my go-to girl for, well...for just about everything and anything, and ever since she left, I've had a big amount of I-miss-yous in my heart for her.

"It just seems like everyone's doing their own thing," I say to Skye, "even today. I thought the festival was going to be about the Pink Ladies rockin' and rulin', except we're all off doing...well, our own thing."

"Festivals are like that, Lola," Skye says, pulling her legs back into the shade. "They're like big bubbles of fun that are protected from the outside world, and there's so much to do that if you stayed together you wouldn't do the things that you wanted to do, or see the bands you wanted to see..."

"I guess," I say, trying to smile, before taking a big bite from a big chunk of the chocolate cake. It's good. Really good.

"Lullah and I used to come to this festival every year," Skye says, pushing her fringe out of her eyes with her sunglasses.

"Really?" I say, my mouth too full of yummy cake to elaborate.

"Really!" Skye says, laughing at me. "One year, we blagged our way backstage by bringing guitars. We figured that if we walked in with a really recognisable act, carrying an instrument, we'd look just like we were with the band – it only worked! The security guards never questioned us or anything, and we had hot showers and hung out with cool boys in bands all weekend!"

I love hearing stories about Aunt Lullah; it makes me feel all warm and fuzzy.

"I don't suppose you know who they are?" Skye asks, nodding towards a table where three neon-clad girls are talking noisily in Italian. "They look so cool!"

"Ohmystars!" I say, turning away really quickly because I don't want them to think I'm staring. "That's the Piperita Patties, and they're increds, Skye. They're a total MySpace phenomenon, and their songs are like real shouty girl anthems."

"So you're a fan, huh?!" Skye laughs at my Wikipedia-like knowledge of the band.

I start nodding like a toy dog.

"Absolutely!"

"So are you going to interview them for your zine?" she asks.

"Well, no, I wasn't going to," I say, trailing off. "But it would be amazing, wouldn't it?"

"Why not do it then?" Skye says, giving me a gentle push up from my chair. "They look fab; you like them, right?"

I nod.

"Your readers will dig them, right?"

I nod again.

"Well then, go and introduce yourself. You'll kick yourself tomorrow if you don't."

"But I couldn't—" I start.

"Yes you could," Skye finishes.

And you know what? She's right! Yes I could. I'm Lola Love, go-for-it girl. I'm at a festival, I'm backstage and isn't it me who's always saying that if any opportunity comes along, then you should grab it?

So I'm gonna get grabbing. Okay, deep breath, Viva La Diva. I walk tall, I channel Audrey for poise, Marilyn for confidence and Jayne for sassiness and before I know it, I'm hovering by their table.

"Hey!" I say. Maria Luisa, who has pillar box red hair, smiles up at me. I can't even begin to tell you how super-cute these girls are: they're dressed head to toe in neon brights, Hello Kitty accessories and general girly goodness.

"I'm sorry to interrupt, but I just wanted to say I love you guys."

I realise immediately that telling them I love them is not the coolest sentence of words and phrases I could have used. "And I love 'All My Friends are Girls'."

Yep, I say that too, but do you know what? I don't really care, because you should always tell people you dig them, no matter how cheesy or schmaltzy it sounds. I mean, seriously, who wouldn't want to be told they rock?

"So I do a zine for girls and was wondering, if you're free, if I could interview you for it?" I babble before I can run away.

The girls all look at each other and smile.

"Of course. Wow, we'd be honoured. Love your outfit, princess – you look hot! Pull up a chair!"

Turning around, I give Skye a quick thumbs-up and pull up a chair next to Maria Luisa.

"So this is my zine." I pull out a copy of my last zine and the girls practically swoon over the pages; I feel myself blush with embarrassment as they flick through. Luckily, as well as blush time, this gives me a couple of moments to think up some questions, but there's so much I want to know about them that I don't struggle at all.

Once I've practically filled my writer-girl notebook with all things Piperita Patties, I tell them about the Rainbow Hearts, give them a copy of our CD and they give me lots of advice.

"It was so great to meet you, Lola," Maria Luisa says, giving me a hug as I finish up. "I wish that every interview was as much fun as this!"

After several more Piperita Patties-flavoured hugs, I practically bounce back to Skye, who has been tapping into the free backstage wi-fi. See, backstage really is like the real world.

"So how was it?" she says, clicking away on her tiny keyboard. "You seemed to be having fun!"

"It was awesome, Skye! They're awesome – thanks for kicking my bee-hind," I say, still a tiny bit in shock.

"I didn't do anything," Skye replies, closing up her laptop. "You're the one that went over there; I'd never have done what you just did at your age – I would've been way too shy."

Now you tell me, I think to myself happily. There's nothing like being a go-for-it girl to give yourself a case of the happies.

"Ohh, it's Ohh-la-la Aimee!" I say pointing to the noise in the air.

"Shoot, is it?" Skye hastily swallows her last mouthful of lemonade. "Gosh, thank god you're here, Lola, I said I'd review her set for the magazine, quick lets go!"

"Go where?" I asked.

Skye looked at me as if I was a tiny bit simple. "Backstage, of course."

Of course.

Chapter Fifteen

One minute I'm interviewing the Piperita Patties, the next, I'm at the at the side of the Electro stage watching Ooh-la-la Aimee in an all-in-one Lycra catsuit marching up and down the stage and singing about French boys who have treated her badly.

I take a peek at the audience. The Rainbow Hearts were worried about playing in front of a hundred or so people at the *Missy* roadshow but that was nothing compared to this. The crowd stretches right back as far as the fun fair that we walked past this morning and they're all cheering and dancing and singing; it must be an amazing feeling to know you can rock a crowd like that.

Even the people at the side of the stage are dancing. Across the stage from me, I can see Bella with the ma-parental. I check my phone to see if they reminded me to come see the show with them and I missed their call or text, but there's nothing from them. Hmm. But there is a text from Angel saying that she's hanging out with the fash pack discussing next season's colours.

I look up to see Bella grabbing the ma-parental's arm and making her dance. They look the way a mother and daughter would look in my dreams: all happy and smiley. Instead of getting a messy stressy head, I turn my attention to Ooh-la-la Aimee, who is stomping around the stage in her trademark six-inch platforms, and try to concentrate on her performance. There is a go-for-it girl if ever I saw one, and I figure I'll go and join Bella and The Mothership after the set, but when I look aver at the stage again, they've vanished.

"So what did you think?" Skye asks, as a sweaty, out-of-breath Ooh-la-la Aimee runs past us.

"Of what?"

Of the fact that Bella and the ma-parental are a better mother/daughter combo than the Lola and the ma-parental combo ever has been? That we said we'd meet after the fashion show and they just came without me?

"Of Ooh-la-la Aimee," Skye gives me that look again. "Come on Lola, you're my barometer of all things super-cool."

I am? Blush x 1000.

"Well, I really like her style – she's definitely brave, but I don't know if she's doing anything *that* exciting," I say thoughtfully. "It's nothing new is it? It's just electro pop with fun lyrics."

"That's what I love about you, Lola – not one to follow a trend!" Skye smiles. "You're absolutely right of course. That's why I wouldn't put her on the cover even though all the advertisers are going crazy. But I have promised to do a fest special with her."

"Ahh, that's what Angel was talking about earlier – she read about it on those fashion blogs," I nod.

"Oh, I know," Skye throws her hands up into the air. "Apparently, they were going crazy, making up stories about how we were now having a fierce battle – geddit? *Fierce*? The things is, I don't read them Lo-Lo. I just don't care what other people think. What if I read them and then my vision was swayed? At least if I stay totally focused on what I'm trying to do, random people's thoughts and opinions won't influence mine."

"But then how would you ever find new talent or discover new things?" I ask. I see what she means – I always try not to let other people's opinions affect mine – but it's really hard not to, and I don't even run the world's coolest fashion magazine.

"Well, I do listen to people, Lola, but only to the people I trust. You know what I'm trying to do with *Fierce*. I don't want it to be full of people the advertising team think should be in it. I want it to be full of people that deserve to be in it. Like those girls you were talking to earlier; what were they called?"

"The Piperita Patties?" I say excitedly.

"They would look awesome on the front cover," Skye muses, her brain clearly ticking over at a million miles an hour.

"Hey, Skye Summers, are you trying to out-scoop me?" I ask, mock-shocked. "Because *Think Pink* has an exclusive there!"

"Ha! You got me, Lola – how about you hook me up with an intro, and I'll let you come to the photoshoot when we arrange it?" Skye laughs.

Smiling right back, I give her a double thumbs-up.

"Ed-girl, you have a deal."

Chapter Sixteen

Not only am I now an honorary Piperita Patty (I am, y'know – they said so) I'm now also talent-spotter for *Fierce* magazine.

Go me.

After setting up dates in diaries with their manager, Skye has to head back to Londinium and the Piperita Patties have to go back to their tour bus to do one final rehearsal, leaving me footloose and buddy free. I text my Pink Ladies to find out what they're up to, but after ten reply-free minutes I realise that I'm flying solo.

Still, even if I'm on my own in this one, I really want to see the Piperita Patties perform. It's their first ever UK gig but I've seen them on YouTube and they're wild. All hot pink lips, dangerous dresses and killer heels, plus they're shouty and raw and passionate – forget Ooh-la-la Aimee and her stylized tunage; I want to be in *their* gang!

Given my new cooler-than-cool press pass, I could watch them from the side of the stage but I'd be on my own: I want to be where the action is, down the front.

It's cool, I can do this, I tell myself. *I can totally do this.*

I leave the comfort and cleanliness of the backstage area (yes, I did use the loo before I left. They had plush toilet roll and everything) and make my way round to the front of the stage. It's starting to get dusky and there's a real party atmosphere, as people dance, hold hands and generally go crazy on the happy vibes in the main arena. I totally get the festival thing now. It's a total escape from reality.

I've got fifteen minutes before the band come on so I hop into the queue for a cheeseburger (look, I couldn't resist, okay?) and despite there being a million, trillion strangers all around me, I manage to bump straight into one of Alwyn's cowboys.

"Hey, you're camping with Bella," he says, offering me a pink lady-like high five.

I high five him right back, glad to see a friendly face. "I do," I reply. "I'm Lola."

"Jonny," he says, giving me a big old grin before turning his attention to the important business of reviewing the burger menu.

"So have you met Bella before?" I ask.

Jonny nods. "Yeah, Hamish and Loretta, they're Alwyn's parents, they've been friends with Bella's dad since Bella was little, I think. They used to meet up at festivals all over the world but I think Alwyn finally talked them into staying in one place for longer than five minutes."

I nod along, although I'm really thinking how cool it would be to travel all the time. I mean, I love my pink palace but Dullsville-by-the-Sea is no match for the big wide world.

"I'm glad, really, that he's hanging in one place for a while – he's such a cool guy," Jonny carries on. "I was a total loser before I met him; no one would talk to me at school."

"No way!" I can't believe it. Jonny's so cool, it almost hurts my eyes to look at him. He's tall with lots of dark blonde hair and, not that I noticed, really beautiful blue eyes. There's no way this boy is unpopular.

"No, seriously," he laughs. "We can't all be born as cool as you, Miss Pink Hair! I was tall and lanky and stood out for all the wrong reasons, but then one day Alwyn walks into my class and he just sits down right next to me and says 'Hey, I'm Alwyn, I'm a world explorer,' and I knew we were going to be buds."

I try not to blush at his first comment – he thinks I'm cool?!

"That's so weird, I was just the same when I met Bella," I say. "I was so jealous of the idea of waking up somewhere different all the time, but she just wants to settle down. And I was so not cool before I met her. She was the one who dyed my hair pink."

For a brief heartbeat, I have a melty moment for Miss Bella. She really has done loads for me.

"I think your hair's ace!" Jonny says, ruffling my candyfloss-coloured locks and giving me another one of those grins.

"Thanks, Jonny," I grin right back. "And I think the fact that you're tall is going to be all kinds of helpful when we want to get to the front of the crowd, right?"

"You would hope so!" he laughed. "There has to be some benefits to being this tall. Except I've lost everyone. We were all supposed to meet before Ooh-la-la Aimee but I just couldn't find them."

"Me too," I say, "I mean, we were all meant to see the Piperita Patties but I don't know where anyone is."

"Oh, are they on next?" Jonny asks. "I really want to see them! I've heard they're really good. Aren't they Italian?"

"Yes, yes, yes!" I yell, jumping up and down. How cool is this boy? "Maybe we should just go and see them?"

Jonny holds out his hand. "Lets go!"

As you would expect, The Piperita Patties rock the stage and I realise how much fun it is to be hanging out with a boy-type again. It's not in an 'I-want-to-smooch-you' way, because Oscar is still my partner in smooch even if he's not around, but it's not in an Ooh-la-la Charlie kind of way either, because he'd never jump up and down in a mosh pit with me for fear of ruining his shoes or his hairdo. It's just a coolio-a-go-go-boy-bud kind of a way and that is just fine with me.

Halfway through the set, Maria Luisa takes the mic and yells out to the crowd.

"We wrote this one literally half an hour ago, after we met this really cool girl with pink hair, so we wrote a song about her. It's called 'We heart Lola Love!'"

I'm not even joking.

That's exactly what just happened.

Jonny turns to me and gives me a big, wide-eyed look.

"That's you, isn't it?" he asks.

I nod, trying not to blush the same colour as my hair.

"I'll explain on the way back!" I say, listening to everyone around me cheering for a song that's written about me.

"You're so rad, you'd be right to think this song is about you! You're so cool, pink hair, pink lips and pink beret! Pink rocks, you rule, Lola Love, we heart you!" the Piperita Patties sing together. It's fast, it's punchy and it makes people smile.

A song about me.

Officially the new theme tune to *Livin' La Vida Lola*.

Chapter Seventeen

The Piperita Patties do not disappoint. Fact.

As the crowd splits and people make their way back to their temporary homes on the hill, I am still singing 'All My Friends Are Girls' at the top of my voice with my new boy-bud Jonny.

"They were amazing, weren't they?" I manage in between verses.

"*They* were, Lola," Jonny says, holding his arm out for me to link mine through. "However, unfortunately, *you* are not. This band you told me about, The Rainbow Hearts, you don't sing, do you?"

I give him a playful tap. I've known him for literally the length of a Piperita Patties playlist and he's being the cheeky chico from Cheekyville High.

"I'll have you know," I tell him, as we make our way through the crowds, "my voice is really rather lovely."

"Oh I know," he says, gently nudging me around a group of people who are *never* going to make it back to their tent. "I hear you're really popular with deaf cats – they love your work!"

"Oh really? Well, ring, ring," I say, making a pretend phone from my thumb and little finger. "I've got Woody from *Toy Story* on the phone and he says he'd really like his outfit back!"

"I don't look like Woody!" he pouts. "I'm like those proper

cowboys, y'know, like from the black and white movies..."

"Of course you are, Jonny," I say giving him a wink, "of course you are..."

Hanging with Jonny is all kinds of fun, and while he *is* really rather nice to look at, he's not Oscar. Sweet, adorable, my real-actual-boyfriend Oscar. For a moment, I wish Oscar were with me. He would have known exactly what to say and do about the Bella/Mothership sitch, he would've offered me his hoodie when it got cold (which, FYI, it is right now) and he would've scribbled a cartoon version of The Piperita Patties for my wall, because, well...because he's just like that.

"You okay, Lola?" Jonny asks, wrinkling his forehead at the sudden radio silence.

"Yeah," I say, shaking sad-girl thoughts from my mind, because after all, it's not Jonny's fault that he isn't Oscar – and to be fair to him, I couldn't have found a better example of boy-kind to act as stand-in.

"I'm fine. So are you ready to come in at the chorus?"

"No!" Jonny pleads, putting his hands to his ears. "No, Lola please, seriously, no more!"

Obviously I totally ignore him and continue to sing 'All My Friends are Girls' at the top of my voice, at which he just shakes his head.

Despite his inability to spot incredible talent right when it's under his nose, I have never been more pleased to have met a cowboy called Jonny because how I would ever have found my way back to Casa Bliss without him, I do not know. It took half an hour and about eight wrong turns before we even came close to finding the pink, leopard-print tent of loveliness and if we hadn't been jumped from behind by a double dose of cuteness in the shape of Sadie and Alwyn en route, it could have been a whole lot longer.

"Lola Love!" Sadie shouts, literally wrapping her arms around my neck and jumping on my back. "I can't believe The Piperita Patties just sang a song all about you; that's crazy-exciting!"

"Did you see the show too then?" I ask, pulling her up by the legs so she's riding piggy-back (or Lola-back). "Weren't they amazing? I think I've bored poor Jonny to tears with my Piperita Patties talk!"

Jonny, who has Alwyn on his back, gives me a wink. "Not at all, Lola!" he says, pretending to struggle under the weight of his barely-there bud. "I don't think you've mentioned them or sung one of their songs once the whole way home!"

"Ha! The set was pretty awesome though, wasn't it?" Sadie says in my ear. "We ran down after the workshop – which was increds, Lo – and we tried to find you, but there were just so many people!"

"Not to worry," I tell her, bumping her up above my hips to stop her falling. "Woody...ahem, I mean Jonny kept me company."

"Right, that's it Lola – you've asked for it now," Johnny shouts. "Alwyn, hold on tight; we're about to race these girls back to camp – losers have to make the baked bananas!"

No sooner has Jonny announced that the race is taking place, he and Alwyn are speeding ahead up the hill, in and out of tents, making pretend lasso actions at random people and things.

Très embarrasmondo.

I grab Sadie tight and try to keep up, but it's not really a fair competition as Jonny is really tall and has legs twice the length of mine.

"So, Sades," I say, following the cowboys' trail of disruption back to camp, "you had fun with Alwyn?"

"Oh, Lo-Lo," Sadie says, her voice turning to caramel swirls of swoon, "he's so lovely – he introduced me to people, he gave me loads of compliments about my drumming, and then, on the way down to the main stage, he held my hand like it was a completely okay thing to do, and it was, but Lo, we were holding hands! Y'know, like boyfriend and girlfriend or something!"

"That's so cool, Sadiecakes," I smile. "You look like cuteness personified when you're together!"

"Really?" Sadie asks. I can't see her, but I can feel she's blushing as her cheek rests on the side of my head. "Well, I really like him, Lola. Although I never thought I'd fall for another drummer – I thought my heart was only for the guitar-toting Tooties!"

"Well, there's your proof that you should never limit your choices, in life or in choosing boy-types," I tell her, secretly pleased that I'm the one who gets to give out the advice once in a while. "If you only ever ate vanilla ice-cream, just think of all the other yummy flavours of ice-cream you'd miss out on, like cookies and cream, chocolate, caramel and coconut...and that's just for starters!"

"You're right," Sadie laughs and slides down off my back. "Trust you to think of life in ice-cream flavours, Lo-Lo!"

"In my world, Sadie, that's the only way *to* think," I tell her, before grabbing her hand. "Look, there's the tent! Let's go!"

Chapter Eighteen

"Beat you!" Alwyn and Jonny say in unison, looking suitably smug when Sadie and I finally make it back to our little area of outdoor living.

"Yeah," I say in a really bad Americano accent. "Yeah you did, you're officially the fastest cowboys in the west."

"Yeee-haaarrrr!" the boys yell, spinning their pretend lassos in the air. Sadie and I play their silly game and pretend we've been caught, falling to the floor with a bump.

"You kids had fun?" Yoga Dad asks, looking up from the rather impressive campfire he's built. There really is no end to his skills.

"Lots and lots, thank you!" I tell him, because even though I didn't think I would, I did. "Except I've managed to lose Angel – have you seen her?"

"I'm here!" Angel sings, flipping open the tent flap like it's a curtain on the West End stage. "Lola, where did you get to? I sent you a text. Chris brought me back up here on a golf cart – it was hilarious! He's such a dollface. Can you believe he introduced me to Vivienne Sui? I thought I was going to throw up, I was so excited!"

"Gosh, Angel," Sadie says, sitting up and turning to face her. "You didn't, did you?"

"Of course not, Sadie!" Angel tuts. "I just said I *thought* I was going to. Gosh, can you imagine? I would have died!"

"Did you actually speak to her?" Bella asks, following her out of the tent, armed with a bunch of bananas and tin foil.

"I did!" Angel says excitedly, rubbing her hands together. "And guess what she said?"

We all shake our heads as Angel builds the tension to her story in her totally Angel, typical drama-queen style.

"She said," Angel continues, adding a few extra pauses for dramatic effect, "that I had made an interesting fashion choice for such an event and she applauded my ability to 'play' with fashion."

"Wow!" I say, super-excited for my BFF to meet one of her idol-girls. "Did she ask you to be in her next catwalk show with Ooh-la-la Aimee?"

"Sadly, no," Angel says, a little disappointed. I only meant it as a joke, but I know how Angel's mind works – she would see no reason why she shouldn't be in the next Vivienne Sui show and I love her for that.

"So how was Ohh-la-la Aimee?" Angel asks Bella. "From what I heard backstage at the fashion show, she's a complete diva!"

We all laugh at Angel because hearing her call someone else a diva is just funny x 100 but she gives us all her trademark Angel glare, which just makes us laugh even harder.

"Well," Bella says, pulling a face, "Angel heard right, didn't she, Pops?"

"I couldn't possibly comment," Yoga Dad says gently as he wraps each banana individually in tin foil. "I just think we need to send her lots of nice thoughts as she is obviously not a very happy person."

"Which," Bella says, rolling her eyes at Yoga Dad, "translated into non-spiritual speak, means 'Yes, she was a nightmare, but I'm a nice person so won't say anything bad about her', doesn't it, Pops?"

"No, Bella," Yoga Dad says, placing each banana onto the grill that he's set up over the fire. "I meant what I said. I think when people get fame too quickly, they don't know how to channel it positively and it affects them. I see it a lot..."

"So, Angel," Bella says, giving Yoga Dad a loving touch on the shoulder, "basically, she wasn't awful, but she wasn't really nice either. It was just a bit sad because I love her music and she just wasn't what I wanted her to be."

"She's only human, I guess," Sadie says, snuggling under a purple blanket with Alwyn. "She can't be everything to everyone all the time. Gosh, that would just be exhausting. Who knows? She might just have been having an off-day."

"No, you're right," Bella says, poking at the bananas to see if they're ready. "I just can't help being a little bit...disappointed, I guess."

As the boys throw their opinions into the mix, The Mothership calls me over to where she's brewing up nettle tea on the camper van stove. Yes, you heard correctly.

My ma-parental. Nettle Tea.

Actually, it's really quite nice and really good for the digestive system but even I'm still in shock at how The Mothership has embraced Yoga Dad's alternative lifestyle.

She offers me a chipped mug and fills it to the brim with tea. I blow on it to cool it down as she fills herself a mug, and we sit on the stair of the camper van, away from the buzz of the group.

"I missed you today, Lola," The Mothership says, taking a sip of tea and putting her hand on my knee. I want to say 'well, it didn't look like you were missing me *that* much when you were pulling shapes at the side of the stage with Bella', but I don't. Instead I smile, and ask her how her day has been.

"Gosh," she says, hugging her mug with both hands, "I could have done with you for moral support – Bella's like a whirlwind!

We went to a tent where there was a talk about macrobiotics – it's a way of life, apparently Lola – well, I don't mind telling you I was bored after five minutes!"

I smile, secretly quite pleased that I still know my own parental better than Bella does.

"And then," the ma-parental continues, rolling up her sleeve, "we got a henna tattoo. Again Bella's idea; what do you think?"

It's a swirly Indian design that's all over the back of her hand and up her arm: it's beautiful.

"It's really pretty, Mum," I say, tracing the pattern over soft skin.

"Hmm, I'm not so sure," she says, pulling her sleeve back down, "but I just think it's sweet that Bella's trying. Maybe you could hang out with her dad for a while... You do like him, Lola, don't you?"

"Of course I do!" I say, because I do, I really, really do. He's the nicest man you will ever meet. I'm just not altogether sure about him being *my* Yoga Dad, that's all.

"And you're okay with everything else?" she asks, rubbing my shoulder.

I want to say yes, because I've got no reason not to be; I want to say no, because the big bunch of weird that's in my belly says I'm not happy, and yet I don't say anything, because I can't find the words to describe this big bunch of weird. So instead I change the subject.

"So," I say, trying to be as bright and cheery as I can possibly be, "I met Lullah's friend Skye today – she's just got back from visiting her in New York. Sounds like they had so much fun! And Skye took me backstage and I met the Piperita Patties who are this amazing girl-group from Italy – I interviewed them for my zine and then they sang a song about me on stage! It was the best fun!"

"It sounds like it!" the ma-parental says, smiling. "You see what happens when we both try new things, Lola? It's okay, isn't it?"

I don't know whether she's asking me or telling me, but she's smiling. It's weird because the ma-parental is almost talking like

Lullah, and now that she's stopped fretting and smiles more, you can really see the sister-like resemblance.

"Lola!" Bella shouts across the campfire. "Vote Pedro and the Rainbow Hearts are going to perform an impromptu set – can you get the guitar out of the van please?"

"Okay!" I shout back, reaching behind the ma-parental to get Bella's rock-girl red and black guitar. I don't know why, but I give The Mothership a kiss on the cheek. She smiles a big smile and I feel my own face stretching into the same shape.

The impromptu collab between Vote Pedro and The Rainbow Hearts is beginning to pull quite a crowd. We sing and play songs that both bands know, like 'I'm a Rockstar' by The Tootie and 'Girl Meets Cake' by Kelk and the Skinny Jeans – Sadie and Alwyn beat out the rhythm on a set of bongos, Jonny and Bella play their guitars and sing, while Angel and I shake tam-tams that we made with Loretta's help using rice and paper plates.

The crowd seems to like the mish-mash of sound that we're making, and they clap and whoop at the end of every song. We all exchange smiles because we are literally getting claps for having fun. It's no wonder people become pop stars – I'm positively giddy from the feel-good loveliness.

Seriously, if someone – anyone – had tried to tell me that today would have been filled with a fashion show, Skye Summers, backstage at Ooh-la-la Aimee, interviewing the Piperita Patties, them singing a song about me, and now this, I would never, ever have believed them.

I mean, who knew camping could actually be fun?

Chapter Nineteen

✳ ✳ ✳ ✳ ✳ ✳

Reasons camping rocks

Baked bananas – dee-lish.

Singing around a campfire – cliché? Maybe. Cool?
Deffo.

Chatting with your gal-pals 'til way past 2am in the

morning – an outside slumber party really is the best kind

of slumber party.

Being able to see a gazillion stars in the night sky coz

you're in a field. In the middle of nowhere. With mud.

"Is it morning already?" I say, shielding my eyes from the light that's coming in through the tent flap.

"It is indeed, *mon amie!*" Bella says, already up and dressed in a rather un-Bella-like cute ensemble of purple tights, a pink and white ra-ra skirt and long purple cardi.

"What's going on?" I ask, looking over to see Angel and Sadie still tucked up in their sleeping bags, with their eye masks pulled firmly over their faces. "Where you going? What you doing?"

"Well," she says, pulling her purple cardigan in at the waist with a red cinch-in belt, "I got up to do early morning sun salutations with Pops, had a shower and now I'm taking your mom to have her tarot cards read. Then we're heading down to the main stage to see some bands, want to come?"

Actually, I do rather fancy having my tarot cards read, but it'll take forever to get ready and as cool as I am with Bella waking me up to see if I'll tag along, I still don't know how cool I am with hanging out *avec* Bella and The Mothership in a family unit sort of way. Maybe when we're back home I'll be able to process all these crazy-swirly feelings.

"That's sounds cool," I yawn for affect and snuggle back into my sleeping bag, "but I'm still super-sleepy. Why don't you text me when you're ready to go watch some bands?"

"Okay, Lo-Lo," Bella shrugs and turns to my mum, who looks over, a little concerned. I give her the biggest smile and wave I can manage, then watch as the two of them make their way off to the Soul and Spirit field.

Without me.

"Hey Lola," Yoga Dad calls from what looks like exactly the same position as we left him in last night, crouched beside the campfire. He's a total nature boy and looks completely at ease as he fills a pan with baked beans.

"Did you and the girls want some breakfast?" he asks, gently stirring the beans with a wooden spoon. "I'll have one beans on toast right here, ready in a sec."

I look back inside the tent and see that there's no movement from either of them – they must have ear plugs in as well as eye-masks on, because camping out with hundreds of other people is not a quiet affair.

"They're not up yet," I whisper-shout in his direction.

"Well, how about you then?" he asks. "Are you hungry?"

I check in with my stomach. The baked banana, despite being the yummiest thing I've tasted in a whole lot of forever, seems like a million hours ago now, so a smile creeps across my face and Yoga Dad takes this as his cue to load up the toast.

I climb out of the tent in my pink polka-dot PJs, just as Johnny and the boys are heading to the showers.

"Cute PJs, Lola!" Jonny says with a smile,

"Are you mocking me, Woody?" I smile back, wrapping a blanket that smells of wood smoke from the fire around me.

"Me?" he says, pulling a pretend-offended face. "Never!" He gives me a wink before running to catch up with Alwyn. I pull the blanket around me a little bit tighter and join Yoga Dad at the fire.

The sun is just rising above the hill and, luckily for the mud-allergic (i.e. me), it looks like it might be another nice day. Loretta and Hamish, Alwyn's parents, told us that it almost always rains on at least one of the days and people love to roll and splash in the mud and then they stay that way for the rest of the fest. Maybe I'm just a pink-haired good luck charm. Or maybe the goddesses of good weather know that a rain-free, mud-free festival is really the only kind of festival that will ever be Lola-approved.

"So, what are your plans for today, Lola?" Yoga Dad asks, looking me in the eyes with his own pair of deep blue soul-searchers. When he looks at you, he really does make you feel like you're the only person in the world that actually matters. It's a nurturing and kind feeling, and even if I ever did want to be mad at him – which I don't – but if I did, I just couldn't be.

"I don't really know," I say, looking into the fire and watching the flames lick and swirl around the wood. "I guess I'll wait for the others to wake up and see what they fancy doing. Although I think Sadie said something about her and Alwyn going to do a fairy workshop – I know, don't ask – and Angel said she might take Chris up on his offer of swanky backstage lunch. So I'm not sure yet. Maybe I need to see if there's a programme kicking around somewhere..."

"Okay," Yoga Dad smiles, "but if you find yourself at a loose end, I'd love it if you came along to my session this afternoon; it's with a band..."

"Ohhh, what band?" I ask, more than slightly intrigued.

"I can't really remember the name of them right now," Yoga Dad says. He works with A LOT of celebrity-types so they must all seem pretty similar to him, "but I could always do with an extra pair of hands, if you're free?"

"Maybe," I say, giving him a smile. "Can I get back to you on that please?" It's not that I *don't* want to do it – I'm actually rather keen to find out what other bands indulge in Yoga Dad's magic powers – it's just I don't know what my plans are and as much as I'd like to hang with Yoga Dad, if I can hang out with my gal-pals, then they'll win, hands down. Sorry, Yoga Dad.

"Of course!" He smiles, handing me a plate onto which he puts two slices of toast, covering them in beans and grating a hefty amount of cheese on top. Yum.

"Loretta, Hamish," Yoga Dad says, looking up at Alwyn's parents who are sitting by the fire too, "would you mind giving Lola and I five minutes please?"

Uh-oh. I do NOT like the sound of this.

"Of course," Hamish says, pulling himself out of the deck chair. "We've got to tidy the van anyway – those boys sure know how to make a mess!"

Loretta follows him, leaving Yoga Dad and I in what can only be described as Awkward City, with me suddenly not feeling anywhere near as hungry as I did five minutes ago.

Chapter Twenty

"So, Lola," Yoga Dad says, turning to face me. He's sitting crossed legged and all of a sudden I'm really fascinated by how hairy his toes are. FYI, they're VERY hairy. Ick. "I'm really glad we're getting a chance to talk. You know that I really like your mom, don't you?"

I nod, because I do, and it's nice that he does. Even if it gives me the icks. Like his toes.

"When I met her," he continues, his eyes almost dancing with excitement as he speaks, "it was like she had this imaginary protective armour on, that she'd put up to guard her bruised and battered heart, but after a little while, I started to see through it. Do you know what I'm talking about?"

"Yes?" I say. Because I do. The Mothership's heart probably *was* bruised and battered. But he's missing out the part where my *ears* were bruised and battered from all her shouting.

"And I could see that underneath that tough exterior, there was a beautiful soul who needed, and wanted to be, loved. But I didn't want to rush anything," he continues carefully.

I nod and stare at the grass in front of me. 'Beautiful soul'?

Yoga Dad passes me a little bottle of orange juice. "So, you know, we've been just hanging out, talking, taking things easy until she feels ready to step out of that armour and let herself fall in love again."

Honestly, Yoga Dad makes meeting the ma-parental sound like something Shakespeare would write, y'know, but without all the tragedy and words ending with 'th'. I don't really know what to say.

"I know you already have a dad, Lola," he says, almost reading my mind because I *do* have a dad and I might not know where he is, but I do love him and I miss him, every single day. Even if he doesn't miss me.

"And I don't want to try and replace him, but I'd like for you to know that I'm here for you too, exactly the same way that I am for Bella."

"Um...thanks," I say, because what else can I say? I do want The Mothership to be happy, but I guess, really deep down in my belly, I'm holding on to the hope that someday, she and my dad might get back together. And if she's with Yoga Dad, well...that won't ever happen.

"I think you're a really special girl, Lola," Yoga Dad says, with such love that I feel like he's wrapped me in an imaginary blanket of sweet and positive thoughts, "and I'm honoured that the universe has brought you and your mom into my life."

As schmaltzy as that sounds, Yoga Dad has a way of making even the most 'out-there' stuff sound perfectly okay. And it does. Sound perfectly okay, I mean. Of course I want my dad to come back – but he's not going to. He's gone. If he'd wanted to see me, he'd have written or called the house, but he hasn't.

And if I really do want The Mothership to be happy then I really don't want her and my dad back together. The Mothership + Lola Dad = shouting, screaming and lots and lots of crying. Which made for a very unhappy ma-parental; which made for a very unhappy Lola Love.

I look up at Yoga Dad, who has gone back to cooking his beans. I think it's cool that he's letting me have a moment to chill and think about what he's said, not trying to force me to be okay with it. But then, he's Yoga Dad and Yoga Dad is, if nothing else, cool.

With a big decisive sigh and a giant chug of OJ, I decide that if the ma-parental is cool with having Yoga Dad in our world, then so am I. Officially. But what I'm still having issues with is the multi-functional Bella – Bella as Pink Lady, Bella as big sister, Bella as the ma-parental's new accessory.

Yoga Dad looks up and gives me a searching smile from across the orange and yellow flicker of the fire flames.

"You'll have to forgive Bella," he says, actually reading my mind this time. He is officially magic, like Aunt Lullah. "It's just that she's always wanted a sister...and a mom."

As Yoga Dad speaks, I try to remember a time that Bella and I have spoken about her mum, and I can't. And the reason that I can't is because we haven't. Ever. As spiritual and lovely as Bella can be, she can also be a whole lot of gnarly emotion and when the neon gnarly sign is flashing you know that whatever subject you were about to discuss is a total no-go area. Her mum is deffo one of those subjects.

"Bella never talks about her mum," I say to Yoga Dad, matter-of-factly, as an insta-flash from yesterday of Bella speaking to Hamish and Loretta enters my head.

"No," Yoga Dad says, hanging his head slightly, "she doesn't. Her mom died when she was very young. Hamish and Loretta were there when it happened, which is why we have such a bond with them. It was hard for both of us, but Bella especially."

Woah. Stop all the freakin' presses in the world.
Bella's mum *died*?
Ohmystars, I feel AWFUL x 100000000.
I've been so busy thinking about how all this weirdness is affecting me that I haven't stopped to think for one minute about

Bella. No wonder she wants to hang out with The Mothership so much. I slap my forehead thinking about how selfish I've been.

"Hey," Yoga Dad says, taking my hand, "what are you doing?"

I look at his kind face and realise that the big bunch of weird may still be a big bunch of weird but at least it's not a big bunch of awful. In fact, it's far, far from it.

"I've just been so selfish," I tell him, thinking back to all the horrible thoughts I've had about Bella and The Mothership. "I...I...I just didn't know, and I was upset that they both got on so well, and..."

I hiccup through the tears, and Yoga Dad wraps me in a hug and strokes my hair.

"Oh, Lola," he says in an almost whisper, "all feelings are valid feelings. If you're feeling angry, it's okay to feel angry, if you're sad or jealous it's okay to feel those feelings too. It's when we start taking those feelings out on other people that the problems can start..."

He's right, just like he always is. Just because I'm a Pink Thinker, doesn't mean that sometimes I won't feel glum – it's how I deal with the glum that really matters. Because I'm usually so pink and sparkly, it felt wrong to be sad and angry, but by not been acknowledging my feelings I've become snappy and rude to the people around me – especially Bella, who's done nothing except want to be part of a family: *my* family.

I wipe my tears away and give Yoga Dad a peck on the cheek.

"Thank you," I say, blowing my nose and arranging my face into a shape of normality. "And just so you know, I think it's cool that you and my mum are, you know, hanging out. So um, thank you."

And I mean it. For being so wise, for being so caring and for going completely out of his way to make sure I'm happy even when I'm being a petulant, grouchy girl from Glumsville City.

"Is that offer still on to help you?" I ask, unwrapping myself from the blanket and folding it up.

"Of course," Yoga Dad says with a smile so wide it looks like it might be hurting his face.

"Then count me in!" I tell him. Okay, so he might not be my dad but he's here and he cares and he's got access to the VIP showers.

That's good enough for me.

Chapter Twenty-one

After a hot non-public shower and the use of a non-stinky toilet – okay, so I know I'm not completely living the festival experience but this is *my* festival experience and if it doesn't have to involve unnecessary torment, then it absolutely positively shouldn't – I am washed, dressed and ready to get my bendy-wendy on with Yoga Dad.

As predicted, Sadie is taking Alwyn to the fairy love workshop, which he seems completely cool with – proof, if ever proof was needed, that they are cuteness on a stick of cute. And Angel, dressed in what can only be described as a techno tribal ensemble, with colours so bright and vivid they make my eyes tingle, is going to meet Chris. He wants to introduce her to some of the top names in the London fash pack who are coming down for lunch, sweetie-dahhhling.

That's how he talks. All the time.

We all arrange to meet up later in the day to go see The Tootie, Angel texts Bella with a time and locale so that even if we get lost, or our phones are out of whack, we'll all know that under the red flag by the main stage at four is our meeting point, no matter what we're doing.

The girls and I do a high five and I quickly check my reflection in the shine of the camper van. Personally, I think I'm looking very festival-chic today. I'm rocking a pair of bright pink leggings and a pale blue tasselled tee – like the one I had when I used to go to the beach when I was five – with pink flamingos on the front, accessorized with an assortment of beads and charms. My pink locks may not have been lovingly tended to by my stylist, Miss Bella, today, but I've tied them up with a matching pale blue headband, and do you know what? It looks pretty good.

"Okay, ready!" I shout, as Yoga Dad loads himself up with mats and bags. I offer to help but being the total gentleman that he is, he politely declines. Which is a good thing really, since this ensemble does not scream 'courier' – but, you know, it's polite to offer.

When we reach the entrance gate, Yoga Dad flashes two passes and instantly a security golf buggy pulls up alongside us.

"Hop on, Lola," Yoga Dad says as he unloads all his stuff onto the buggy. "This kind gentleman here is going to take us to our destination."

I feel like a real celebrity as we drive around to the backstage area. People stare, and you can see from the looks on their faces that they're thinking, 'Who are they? What are they doing?'. I practice my best 'who, moi?' face and smile graciously from behind my pink shades. Because that's what Marilyn would do, right?

"So, do you know what band you're going to be working with yet?" I ask Yoga Dad, as we pass the hospitality tent I was sitting in yesterday. Maybe I'll pop back in for that chocolate cake.

"Good thing you're here to remind me to check," he replies, looking in his bag. "I guess I'd better find out before we get there, hadn't I?"

I frown. This is very unlike Yoga Dad. He is usually a details-obsessed kind of guy, always knowing what's going on before it actually happens. Another benefit of having a direct line to the universe, I guess. So for him to not know what's going on, well, that just seems weird to me.

After about five minutes, our driver, Steve, pulls up alongside a big trailer and the familiar sound of my favourite Tootie song, 'I'm a Rockstar' is filling the outside space. Before my brain can put two and two together, my eyes widen and when I turn to Yoga Dad he's smiling at me.

"It's The Tootie, isn't it?" I ask, feeling crazy-excitement bubbling up inside me.

"Yes," he smiles. "Yes, it is. But I need you to be really professional, Lola. I know you've met them before but don't be upset if they don't remember you – it was a while ago, wasn't it? And they meet a hundred different people every day. Is that okay?"

"Yes, I mean, okay, I'll be totally professional, I promise!" I take a deep breath, trying to contain the over-flowing fizz of excitement.

Their trailer is not at all as swank as I'd imagined but it does have a shower room, bunk beds and games consoles, which I guess is all four guys really need. And they must have just sprayed an air freshener before we arrived because it's smelling way too floral for a boy space.

The band members introduce themselves – not that I need any intro to these four boys of total deelish-like yummy stuff – and when it comes to shaking Tom's hand, he hovers, seemingly taking in my entire face.

"Don't we know you?" he asks, a lazy smile stretching across his face.

"Oh, yeah." I try to make eye contact but his eyes are too pretty and I have to look away. "I met you at the *Missy* magazine roadshow."

"*Missy* roadshow?" he repeats, throwing his glance skywards as he looks for a memory. "I got it: you're the zine girl, aren't you? You write a zine... And your band won, didn't they?"

Ohmystars. He does remember me! Tom Tuttie-cutie actually knows who I am. Okay, so he doesn't know my name or anything, but he called me zine-girl. Tom Tuttie-cutie called me zine-girl. Le-blimmin'-sigh.

"Yes, that's me," I say, trying to remain as cool as possible, though under the circumstances this is proving to be way more difficult than it should be, "and yes, I do and er, yes, we did!"

"This isn't going in the zine, is it?" Tom says, looking more than a little concerned.

"Ohmystars, no!" I say, worried that he thinks I'm some undercover journo-girl trying to expose these rock boys as bendy-wendy hippies. "Absolutely, positively, I'm just here to light candles, set up CDs, lay out mats and make sure you have water. If you'd prefer, I'll leave during the actual session?"

"Oh no," Tom laughs, brushing his long fringe from the eyes that make me do an inward swoon, "don't be silly, of course you can stay – just as long as you promise not to laugh at how rubbish we are!"

"You won't be rubbish," Yoga Dad tells him, gently guiding him to the other members of The Tootie while I lay out the mats. "You'll be wherever you need to be, at exactly the right moment you need to be there."

If you're not used to Yoga Dad's wise-isms, I guess they can seem kinda strange, and I catch the boys exchanging an 'uh-oh, what have we let ourselves in for?' look – I know it because it's just like the one that Angel and I pulled at the idea of coming to a festival.

Now, I wouldn't have The Tootie down as yoga kind of boys, and after seeing them warm up, it's quite clear that they're not.

"Look, I'm really sorry," Tom apologises, trying really, really hard to cross his legs into the lotus position, "but our manager thought this would be a really good idea. I've been getting really tense before shows and he'd heard lots of good things about you but... I don't know; look, I'm just not made for this."

The other boys snigger like they're in the back row of history class.

"Don't panic," Yoga Dad says in his soothing voice, "just take it slowly; it's more important that you concentrate on the breathing – in and out, in and out, big deep breaths."

Tom closes his eyes, takes a deep breath in through his nose and blows it out of his mouth. The more he does it, the more his body loosens and the positions become easier for him to do.

And before I know it, I'm concentrating more on how amazing Yoga Dad really is and I'm hardly looking at Tom Tootie even though he's puffing away in the downward dog. Without even breaking a sweat, Yoga Dad has turned four giggly rock boys, who weren't taking it at all seriously, into four peaceful bendy-wendies in the chime of a cowbell.

I sit cross-legged at the side of the room with my eyes closed – I know: who'd have thought I'd actually ever want to shut my eyes if I was in the same room as Tom Tuttie-cutie? But I do, and as Yoga Dad describes a beautiful field that we're walking through, I feel myself there; I feel peaceful, I feel bliss-kissed, I am officially L'il Miss Bliss.

Chapter Twenty-two

"Sadiecakes," I squeal when we all meet under the red flag beside the main stage, "guess what? I met Tom Tuttie and he remembered me!"

"NO WAY!" Sadie squeals a whole ten decibels higher than me. "How did you meet him? Where did you meet him? Tell me everything!"

"Well, the band Yoga Dad was working with were The Tootie," I say, almost fit-to-burst, "except he conveniently forgot to tell me that part... Anyway Tom called me 'zine girl, and, well, it was increds! It was in their trailer so it was a little bit cramped..."

"It was in their trailer?" Sadie squeals at a volume only dogs can hear. "OHMYGOD! What was it like?"

"A bit of a let-down, if I'm honest – *so* not as glam as you'd think," I tell her. "But they were awesome, and Yoga Dad...wow, he was amazing!"

Yoga Dad, who is hand in hand with The Mothership, turns round and mouths the words 'thank you' at me.

"So, what have you been up to?" I ask Sadie, who is scribbling down all of Alwyn's contact details just in case there isn't time later.

"Well, we went to the fairly love workshop," Sadie says, her eyes twinkling like sparkly jewels, "and Alwyn made me a *papier-mâché* version of himself with wings. It's sort of adorable. And then went to see The Boxall Billydogs, who were just crazy-mad, running around the stage, doing cartwheels and making lots of screechy noises with a guitar. We ended up in the mosh pit but because were so small the security guard had to lift us both out – it was brilliant!"

"So, kid," Bella says, putting her arm on my shoulder, "you had hang time with the pops, huh? He's not so bad is he?"

"He's alright," I say, giving him a smile. "Did you have fun with my—with The Mothership?"

Bella gives me a squeeze. "I did – but we wished you had been there. Oh, wait up! Here comes L'il Miss Fashionista!"

We all jump out of the way as a golf buggy comes to a screeching halt beside us.

"Careful!" Angel shouts at the driver. "You'll squash all my bags!"

"Seriously," Bella says, shaking her head, "you're the only person I know who would come to a festival and go home with shopping bags. What have you got?"

"Pink Ladies, I've been blagging!" Angel declares with pride. "I have exclusive Vivienne Sui accessories! Well, when I say I, I mean Chris, obvs; he's my new best friend – I love him!"

"Oh I see," Bella says, putting her hands on her hips, "so you've dropped your old friends for shiny new fashion ones?"

"No!" Angel tuts. "Shiny new fashion friends help me get Vivienne Sui accessories for me AND my Pink Ladies – wanna see?"

Bella never needs asking twice and dives into the bags, pulling out a beautiful plaid print headscarf.

"For me?" she asks, holding it close to her chest like it's the most precious thing she's ever seen.

"For you!" Angel smiles.

Bella lets out a choked sob and gives her a huge hug.

"So tell me," I say, squeezing in between the ma-parental and Bella and linking arms with them both. "What did the tarot card reader predict? Good things I hope – lots and lots of good things?"

"Oh, Lola!" the ma-Parental exclaims in a complete state of shock. "They were her exact words! 'Good things – lots and lots of good things'! That's amazing, how did you know?"

"Well," I say, giving The Mothership a big smile, "maybe I've got a touch of the psychic about me too, just like Aunt Lullah!"

As The Tootie come to the stage and we all let out a massive cheer, I realise that a family isn't always just a mum and a dad, or even a mum, an aunt and a Cattitude; sometimes it's made up of lots of different people. But how many people have a Bella, a Sadie, an Angel, a Yoga Dad and their very own Mothership?

Me and the Pink Ladies finally get our festival on and dance like there's no one watching. Even if there's quite a few thousand people hanging around. Even Yoga Dad and the Ma-Parental are doing a cringey old-people dance at the side of us but it's all kinds of cute. I dive at Bella and give her a big hug, which apparently seems like a good idea to the rest of my Bliss Weekender crew and they all pile into the hug.

These people are my family and I'm incredibly lucky to have them all.

The Pink Zine

Hola!

So, it's official, I heart festivals! I know, I'm as surprised as you are, because I don't mind telling you, chicas, that when Bella's Yoga Dad suggested we join him at the Bliss Weekender, I didn't think it was going to be for me, at all. Although when I found out that the cutie Tom Tuttie was going to be appearing, the idea deffo got a whole lot more appealing!

And camping with your gal-pals rocks, especially when you're sleeping in a totally un-missable pink leopard-print tent – if you're going to do it, you've got to do it in style, right? Although I hope that someday, when the Rainbow Hearts get to play a festival, we'll have a super-cute pink trailer of fabulousness and not have to camp out in a field with nowhere for me to plug my hair straighteners!

So ladies, pitch your pink tent, turn up your iPod and leave your make-up at home – welcome to the Think Pink fest o' fabulousness!

Love and VIP passes...

The Happy List

When your world feels like it's a crumbling biscuit, sit down and make yourself a happy list! Grab some paper, pick a bright coloured marker and write down all the things that make you smile; by the time you're finished, you'll have forgotten what you were unhappy about!

- ❑ Getting snail mail
- ❑ Chocolate milkshakes
- ❑ Laughing so hard my belly hurts
- ❑ Making, and eating, cupcakes
- ❑ Hugs and high fives
- ❑ The Pink Ladies
- ❑ The beach
- ❑ A filled-to-the-brim bubble bath
- ❑ Lying in bed and listening to the rain out side
- ❑ Going on an adventure by reading an awesome book
- ❑ Road trips
- ❑ Watching the sunrise

Baked Banana Bonanza!

When you hang in the fresh air, your appetite will soar, chica. So treat yourself to some yummy campfire home cookin' – deelish.

Ingredients:

1 banana per person
1 marshmallow per person
1 large bar of chocolate
1 tsp cinnamon
Kitchen foil

- Split the bananas down the middle, keeping the skins on.

- Push a few pieces of broken chocolate and a marshmallow into each and sprinkle with cinnamon.

- Wrap the bananas in foil.

- Cook on the campfire or barbecue for about 10-15 minutes.

- Carefully unwrap and eat – Yumsville City!

Happy Campers – The Think Pink survival guide

Pack your best buds, your pink tent and camp it up!

If your tent is as adorably awesome as our pink leopard-print one, you'll want to protect it by:

• Pitching it away from your campfire.

• Not pitching it under trees – lightening hazard!

• Inspecting the pitch area for sharp objects – don't want to be sleeping on anything sharp – ouch!

Don't leave home without...

• A zip-up bag – keep your
stuff secure.

• A fully charged mobile – in
case you lose your gal-pals.

• Wet wipes – instant freshness
– hurrah!

• Padlock – to keep your
belongings safe.

• Toilet roll – goes without
saying really...

• DO keep a pack of tissues in your Hello Kitty rucksack at ALL times.

• DON'T take valuables or favourite clothes – you'll regret it, chicas!

Have a faux-stival!
If you can't afford to go to a festival, don't worry – have your own! Make a playlist of all your favourite bands – mine is over the page – and invite your mates over to camp in your garden. Music, mates and much nicer loos – happy, happy days!

The faux-stival playlist of awesomness!

A mash-up of skinny-jean-wearing guitar boys and shouty-pouty girls – woop, woop!

CSS - Believe Achieve

Blur - Song 2

Gossip - Standing in the Way of
                    Control

The Piperita Patties - All My Friends
                              are Girls

The Killers - Spaceman

Kenickie - Punka

The Strokes - Hard to Explain

Kings of Leon - The Bucket

The Pipettes - Your Kisses are Wasted
                          on Me

Stellastar - Somewhere Across
                    Forever

Sahara Hot Nights - Kicks

One Night Only - Just for Tonight

Make your own tambourine

What faux-stival would be complete with out some crazy tam-tam playin'?! Here's how to make your own!

What you need:

- 2 paper plates

- Stapler and staples

- Glue or tape

- Crayons, markers and coloured pencils

- Magazines, fabric scraps, feathers

- A handful of uncooked beans or half a cup of rice

Instructions:

Place the beans/rice onto one of the plates.

Place the other plate on top Staple the edges of the plates shut – make sure you staple it all the way round, as you don't want the beans/rice to spill out!

Decorate your tam-tam with crayons, markers, magazine clippings, feathers etc...

Wohhooo – you've made your very own tam-tam, now shake it, shake it, shake it like a Polaroid picture!

These girls rock –
The Piperita Patties!

If you love your music in a kitsch, girl-shaped, day-glo fabulous Italian-o package, then you will most deffo love The Piperita Patties!

The PPs – Louie, Marilu and Valeria – are a girl band you can really dig. Their music is bubblecore pop'n'roll with a powerful twist – what could be cooler than that?
Answer? Nothing.

Describe The Piperita Patties in five words...

Marilu: Twist, shout, dance, shortcake, yè-yè.

How did you get together?

M: Well, I'm a specialist in two things: chasing after my teenage dreams and choosing friends... I just put those things together and The Piperita Patties were ready to rock!

What five tunes would be on a PP soundtrack to life?

Louie: Ma Che Freddo Fa (Nada Malanima), Sunday Girl (Blondie), Girls Just Want To Have Fun (Cindy Lauper), Give Him a Great Big Kiss (The Shangri-Las), Dancing With Myself (Billy Idol).

Who are your biggest influences?

Valeria: While playing in the PPs I think about X, the Ramones, DEVO, Blondie, the Muffs...AND Nuggets comps, the Shangri-Las, the Ronettes, the Ikettes, the Chiffons, the Crystals, the Shirelles...

We love girls with attitude – what's your secret to being fabulous?

V: Wow, thanks, fabulous is a gratifying adjective! Marilu is very good in keeping the band together and she always has a lot of brilliant ideas, Louie is usually quiet but she

knows exactly when it's time to quip.
Lately, I'm the master in slopping around...

What's your motto for life?
M: Definitely "IN VOLUPTATE VERITAS" (In
pleasure, the truth).

What were you like as a teenager?
M: A dreamer, an untidy lovely mess...
Pretty much the same as now.

**If you could speak to your teen self, know-
ing what you know now, what advice would
you give her?**
M: Be yourself, express yourself, be
creative, be crazy, be brave, be ahead: it's
what you need to be happy and make
people happy!!!

Check out my favourite band at:
www.piperitapatties.com

Congratulations to Ailsa Winter, aged eleven, from Fife! You're the winner of my Mizz short story Competition!

I picked this story because it took me on a fun adventure that I'd never have thought about creating myself. I loved it!

And congrats to all the other Pink Ladies that entered. Check out Mizz and Lolaland.com for the runners up stories!

Lola x

Lola Love and the Magic Wardrobe

By Ailsa Winter

A never-ending supply of clothes in my wardrobe. That's what I want. Or a door to another world, like in Narnia. My wardrobe's so boring. It's not even pink. I'm Lola Love...

****

"Hi, Lola."

"Oh, hi Sadie."

Lola and Sadie had just arrived at school.

"Look, the laydeebishay," whispered Sadie, "poor Eva. She looks so sad."

"Ignore her. Let's talk about tonight," Lola said.

"I know. We're playing at a concert. A real concert!" cheered Sadie, a little too loud, since she was in school.

"Where are we meeting?"

"How about your house? Five-ish?"

"You could stay for tea. I'll ask my parentals and call Angel and Bella. I hope my parentals will give us a lift 'cos we'll need to take our guitars, drums and mics. Will you bring some make-up?"

Sadie started jumping up and down. "Do you think we'll get a limo?"

"When we're famous."

"When or if?" worried Sadie.

"When!" screamed Lola. Everyone looked at her. Then the bell rang.

"I can't believe we got a gig!" cried Angel.

"Don't you start. I've had enough of this one at school," Lola pointed at Sadie.

"Hey I'm not the only one!" They all giggled.

"Right, make-up's done," said Bella, applying the last of Angel's make-up. They drove to the hall.

"That was the best thing I have ever done!" screamed Sadie. "It was superfantabulous."

"That's not a word," Angel pointed out.

"I know. I just made it up."

"When will we get another gig?" asked Lola.

"We were brilliant. They'll be lucky if we go back there. We had to bring our own equipment," laughed Bella.

"They didn't have mics and drums and guitars," Lola pointed out. "And our guitars are gorgeous."

"True," admitted Bella.

"Did they give you equipment at gigs in America?" asked Angel.

"Well, no," said Bella. "But that was different."

"How?" asked Sadie.

"Fine, you win."

"Let's go home now. I'm tired," moaned Angel. The others looked taken aback.

"I'm kidding," laughed Angel, "but we do have school tomorrow." They packed their equipment and Lola's mum took them home.

A few days later, Lola begged her mum to buy her a pink wardrobe. She compromised and bought her some pink paint. Lola spent her day painting her wardrobe. At night, when she was sleeping, she heard a noise coming from inside.

Slowly, slowly, she crept towards it and gently pushed open the doors. The paint had dried. She swept her clothes to the side and tiptoed inside the wardrobe...

...And out into the land of pink.

"I'm dreaming," she pinched herself. "OW! No I'm not!" Lola gazed at this world. "Where did it come from?"

"It's a present for you, Lola. I'm your fairy godmother. Call me Charlie," said the beautiful, musical voice that was Charlie.

"Okay, Charlie. But why? I mean, all this? For me?" Lola was puzzled.

"Lola, you are the queen of thinking pink," the voice replied. "I have created a land in your pink wardrobe. A land dedicated to you."

"Me?"

"Yes."

"Really?"

"Yes."

"Me?"

"Yes."

"Lola Love?"

"Yes, you, Lola Love."

"Cool. Why?"

"You think pink."

"Cool. Can Angel, Bella and Sadie come?"

"Your best friends are allowed in but only if you want them to see this world. It's your choice. Pink world can be your secret or you can tell them. Only your best friends are allowed in though. No one else. Don't let anyone in that you are not one hundred percent sure that they will always be your best friend. Just them.

No one else."

"You repeat yourself a lot. I think about it, I need my beauty sleep now. Nighty night," said Lola.

"Sleep well," said Charlie.

After a good night's sleep, Lola decided to tell her friends about the land inside the wardrobe.

"Sadie?"

"Yeah?"

"Can you come to my house tonight?"

"Probably. I'll ask the parentals."

"Call me after you've asked."

"Bye." They waved goodbye and walked home from school.

Sadie said that she could come. Lola called Angel and Bella and they said they could come too.

"Hiya, Pink Ladies. I have something to tell you. You have to promise ne that you will never tell anyone. Do you promise?"

"We promise," they laughed and held up their hands like a Guide promise.

"I'm serious."

"So are we." Angel did look serious. Lola opened her wardrobe door.

"This is Pink World. My Pink World. Our Pink World."

"WOW!" shouted Bella, Angel and Sadie at the exact same time. They stepped inside Pink World.

"Hello, girls," said Charlie.

"Who...?" Sadie just noticed how big and beautiful Pink World was.

"That's Charlie, my fairy godmother," Lola said.

Bella was amazed. "Like in Cinderella?"

"Well, yeah."

"Cool!" laughed astonished Sadie.

"I LOVE THIS PLACE!" yelled Angel.

Slowly they wandered around Pink World.

"Is that a massive, pink bar of chocolate?" asked Sadie.

"I think so. Let's try a bit each and see," suggested Lola.

"The piece I took has grown back," Sadie stared at the chocolate.

"Look, pink lemonade!" shouted Bella.

"It's all yours," Charlie told them.

"Look, Grease!" Lola just noticed the gigantic TV.

"It's your own personal cinema."

"Charlie, you're the best. As well as getting all this," Lola looked around. "It's very glam to have a fairy godmother. Very Cinderella."

Sadie asked, "what other films can we watch?"

"It has every chick flick and comedy that you could ever want."

"Really?"

"Yes."

"Really?"

"Yes."

"Cool. Really?"

"Yes."

"Really?"

"Yes."

"Really?"

They all screamed, "Yes!"

"I was just asking," Sadie grumbled.

"Really?" joked Angel.

"Don't you start," warned Lola. "Hey, can you guys stay for a sleepover? We don't have school tomorrow."

"We'll have to call our parentals and ask," said Angel.

Bella told them that she could come and the others were allowed to stay too.

"Does this place have cookie dough ice cream?" asked Bella.

"Of course," said Charlie.

"Look at that dress!" screamed Lola. "Is it for me?"

"Try it on. Those other dresses are for you girls too."

They had a disco under the glitter ball, had a movie marathon and laughed so much that it hurt. They ate so much ice cream and chocolate and pink lemonade that they thought they might burst.

"Those beds?" gasped Lola.

"They're yours," replied Charlie.

"Charlie?"

"Yes, Lola?"

"Will we ever get to see you?"

"Someday. Now go to bed. You love sleeping."

"Bon nuit."

"She speaks French!"

"Nighty night."

"Good night Pink Ladies," said Charlie. They all went to their lovely new, pink beds and fell asleep.

Lola woke up the next morning.

"Woah, who are you?" she asked.

"Charlie," said a girl in her twenties, standing beside Lola's bed.

"Really?"

"Yes."

"Really?"

"Yes."

"Really?"

"Yes."

"But you look young?"

"Thank you."

"You're wearing jeans."

"I know."

"Your hair is purple."

"I know."

"Not grey."

"I know."

"At least you have a wand and a tiara."

"Yes."

"Could your answers be more boring?"

"Stranger things have happened," Charlie smiled.

Lola laughed.

Sadie woke up. "What time is it?" she asked.

"Ten," replied Charlie.

"This is Charlie," said Lola.

"Really?" said Bella.

"Not you too," said Charlie.

"Soz."

"My parentals have muffins for breakfast. I'll go and get them."

Lola came back with muffins and on the table, there was a feast.

"Tuck in," said Charlie. Ten minutes later, there was no food left.

"Charlie?"

"Yes, Lola?"

"I still don't get it. Why me?"

"You think pink and influence others to think pink with you. You and your Pink Ladies deserve it."

"But how did this happen?" Lola asked.

"If you've got the ability to dream something in your head... there is absolutely no reason you can't make it a reality," Charlie explained.

Lola smiled. "I say that. Is this like Narnia? Will the entrance vanish?"

"It's yours forever," Charlie smiled.

Lola looked at her friends. "No Charlie, it's ours forever."

****

We had hundreds of sleepovers in Pink World. This is my fairytale and so I'll end it like one. And they all lived happily ever after...

Hey chicas, join me and the Pink Ladies in our ultimate guides to Thinking Pink!

Are you looking for somewhere fun, fabulous and totally you-nique on the web? Come and hang with me, Bella, Angel and Sadie at Lolasland.com!

We've got news, reviews, interviews as well as beauty, fashion, games and more. You can even build your very own Lola's Land – c'est tres chic!

Looking forward to seeing you there, **chica!**